THE DARK RAVEN

DCI DANI BEVAN 13

By

KATHERINE PATHAK

The Garansay Press

Books by Katherine Pathak

The Imogen and Hugh Croft Mysteries:

Aoife's Chariot

The Only Survivor

Lawful Death

The Woman Who Vanished

Memorial for the Dead
(Introducing DCI Dani Bevan)

The Ghost of Marchmont Hall

A Better Place

Short Story collection:

The Flawed Emerald and other Stories

DCI Dani Bevan novels:

Against a Dark Sky

On a Dark Sea

A Dark Shadow Falls

Dark as Night

The Dark Fear

Girls of The Dark

Hold Hands in the Dark

Dark Remedies

Dark Origin

The Dark Isle

Dark Enough to See

The Eye in the Dark

The Dark Raven

Standalone novels:

I Trust You

This is a work of fiction. Names, characters, businesses, places, events and incidents are either the products of the author's imagination or used in a fictitious manner. Any resemblance to actual persons, living or dead, or actual events is purely coincidental.

All rights reserved. No part of this publication may be reproduced in any form or by any means - graphic, electronic, or mechanical, including photocopying, recording, taping or information storage and retrieval systems - without the prior permission in writing of the author and publishers.

The moral right of the author has been asserted.

© Katherine Pathak, 2021

#TheDarkRaven

Edited by: The Currie Revisionists, 2021

© Cover photograph Unsplash Images

Prologue

The torrential rain which had been falling continuously for days had turned the entrance road a slick black. A procession of buses were inching slowly through the bottleneck that had formed around the formidable iron gates.

The man they called, 'Taff', dared to wipe a tiny circle in the grimy condensation which had made the bus window beside him almost opaque. He peered through the tiny smear of cleaner glass, squinting beyond the mesh covering the outside of the window, thinking it reminded him of a porthole on one of the merchant ships he'd served on in his younger days. Indeed, they suddenly began rocking from side-to-side as those vessels had often done in the rough seas of the Atlantic. This time, Taff felt a deep sickness in the pit of his stomach at the motion, which he'd never done when actually on one of the ships themselves, having gained his 'sea-legs' much sooner than many of his contemporaries.

Through his eyehole, he could see a mass of faces, anger etched upon each one, so that they no longer resembled the human beings he had once known, perhaps even called friends. He felt in his very soul the swell of pure hatred focused upon himself and his fellow passengers. Taff had travelled around the world in his time, but never witnessed loathing such as that burning in the eyes of these men. He swallowed hard against the dry lump lodged in his throat.

The bus lurched forward and then came to an abrupt halt. They were surrounded on all sides. Despite the unseasonal cold of the day, Taff felt the sweat trickling down his back. He could hear the driver shouting and cursing, raising his fists and beating the steering wheel in frustration. A palpable unease was emanating from his fellow passengers. They were trapped in this tin can with windows. It wasn't the sort of bus that had an opening sun-roof, like the coaches his mammy used to take on day trips to the coast with her pals, to walk along the promenade at Bray, enjoying a half of stout in one of the seaside bars, sheltered from the inevitable breeze whipping in off the roiling Irish Sea.

Even if they could've climbed out, where would they go? Outside, were an angrily expectant, merciless crowd with projectiles and possibly even a few home-made Molotov cocktails or two. Was this going to be the end for all of them? Battered and kicked to death by a crazy mob, or worse. Trapped in a burning tin coffin with no means of escape?

Taff sensed a movement in the crowd. He pressed his face up to his spy hole, desperate to see what was going on. The mob was splitting apart, another focus distracting their attention for just a moment. Their driver must have spotted an opportunity as he suddenly jumped on the accelerator, moving them forward when a gap formed and the road ahead was clear. They kangaroo hopped along this way for several more yards.

Then the bus jerked to a halt with a more violent lurch. Taff feared the driver had stalled in his desperation to get away, or perhaps one of the rocks being hurled around outside had hit them, preventing their progress. But the engine kept rumbling on, and the driver must have calculated any damage could be assessed later. They proceeded through the tall gates, away from the baying crowd and towards safety.

Taff shoved his head between his knees so he

couldn't be seen. He realised then that his jeans were damp with sweat and his heart was hammering like a drill in his chest. The man recognised just how close they'd come to a terrible fate at the hands of people he just didn't recognise any longer. He began shaking with relief, or maybe shock. They may have made it through this time, but he was still trapped in a nightmare, where every choice he made had consequences that were simply unthinkable.

Chapter 1

Snow was falling in pretty swirls onto the pavements of Bath Street in Glasgow. DCI Dani Bevan pulled up the hood on her woollen coat and tried to feel festive. She'd been on duty until an hour ago and this was her last chance to buy her Christmas presents. The canopy of fairy lights had just flickered on above their heads and she could smell chestnuts roasting on a street stall somewhere nearby.

Despite these signs of festivity, the city centre seemed quiet to Dani. She didn't believe there were many last-minute Christmas present buying merchants like her any longer. Her DS, Andy Calder, said that his wife, Carol, completed her Christmas shopping online, no later than November. Apparently, if she didn't act early enough, little Amy wouldn't get the toy she really wanted and life wouldn't be worth living at home.

Dani smiled to herself. She only needed to pop into Waterstones in Sauchiehall Street to get a book for her dad. Then maybe a bottle of whisky each for Rhodri and Jim. She'd already sent flowers to James's mum. They were spending Christmas Day with them tomorrow, so Dani wanted some token to arrive ahead of time. She *had* been organised in this respect.

The real obstacle was a gift for James. It was an element of relationships she still found perplexing. They were both professional adults. If there was something they wanted to buy, they'd get it themselves, thus ensuring the colour, or size, or design was exactly to their liking.

Gifts for a partner could be a minefield. Spend too much or too little and you were risking trouble, let alone the nature of the gift itself. Dani sighed. She stared up at the sky, watching the tiny white flakes falling from the blanket of grey above. The phone in her pocket buzzed. The screen lit up as she swiped right.

"Hi James, I managed to finish up early. I'm shopping."

"I know I'm supposed to be deeply impressed, but at 5pm on Christmas Eve that's not something to boast about."

Dani chuckled. "There have been plenty of years when I've been at my office in Pitt Street on the 25th December. Different rules apply."

"Okay, DCI Scrooge, point taken."

Despite the joshing, Dani sensed an edge to James's voice. "Is everything okay? Is it your mum?" Linda Irving had been given the all-clear for her cancer a year earlier, but the family remained on high-alert for any changes.

"No, Mum's fine, don't worry about that. Sally is planning to do all the cooking tomorrow, so she'll not have to lift a finger."

"I'll help too," Dani muttered, thinking of all the Christmases she'd spent with her father on Colonsay, both of them sharing the cooking and baking. She wasn't the complete domestic disaster that others seemed to assume. "So, what is it then?"

There was a pause on the line. Dani could hear James taking a breath. "Do you remember Bernard Raven?"

"Your client who's in construction? I thought you'd already signed off on his latest submissions to the council?" Dani wondered why they were discussing one of the clients from James's legal firm on a freezing Christmas Eve, with snow on the way and urgent shopping to be done.

"Yes, I have. But there are many more submissions to come. Raven Homes are planning a series of new housing estates across Scotland, taking advantage of the government's new mass building project."

"Yes, I know all this, James. My feet are starting to feel like ice-blocks." Dani stamped her court shoes against the pavement to try and get her circulation kick-started.

"He's invited us to a house-party between Christmas and New Year."

"Oh, okay. Well I've got plenty of leave owing, so that shouldn't be a problem. Do you want me to buy them some gifts whilst I'm here in town?"

"Yes, that would be great. But I'm not sure you're grasping my full meaning. The party lasts *from* Christmas *until* New Year. We're invited from Boxing Day until New Year's Eve, when there will be a Hogmanay Ball, apparently."

A couple walking along the street beside Dani gave her a quizzical look as she let out a booming laugh. "Christ! Who the hell wants guests in their house for that long? Especially people they hardly know! You're joking surely?"

James's voice had gone quiet. "No, I'm afraid I'm not joking. The kind of people who have week-long house parties at Christmas, are the types who own a castle in the Highlands."

Dani was straining now to hear her partner's voice above the tinny rendition of carols being produced by a speaker outside one of the shops. She thought she'd picked up on something about Highland Castles. "Have you just got back from your firm's Christmas lunch? Had one too many snowballs?"

"No, darling. This client is huge for us and he

seems to have taken a great shine to me. A select few of Raven's business associates and their partners have been invited. If the weather holds out, he's sending a chopper to pick us up from his pad in Edinburgh the day after tomorrow. If it's not safe to fly, he'll transport us in one of his fleet of four-by-fours."

"Where exactly is this castle of his?"

"Ullapool."

Dani pictured the seaside town of Ullapool, further north even than Inverness, beautiful yet remote, especially in the cold, merciless Scottish midwinter. "Bloody hell." She glanced about her at the warming, inviting soft light spilling from the windows lining the parade of shops, where the snow had settled lightly, producing a shimmering carpet covering the pavements. "At least that sorts out our present choices for this year. Thermal underwear all round."

Chapter 2

A Christmas tree had been placed by one of the windows. It was artificial and had LED lights already attached. The interminable flashing reminded DI Dermot Muir too much of the 'blues and twos' to be festive. In fact, it was giving him a headache.

He'd moved the contents of his desk into the DCI's small office which had the benefit of a miniature electric heater positioned down by the feet. It was one of the perks of rank he supposed. He turned it on at the wall, feeling the blissful pump of hot air, whilst hoping it wouldn't give him chilblains.

He glanced at the clock. It was 11am on Christmas Day. There wasn't another soul on the floor of the Serious Crime Unit. All police officers had to take the Christmas shift every couple of years, it was a part of the job. A handful of his colleagues were due in later, some of them were unmarried or without kids and used the prospect of a quiet festive shift or two to secure a better holiday package in the summer. It made sense to Dermot, if not to his fiancée, Serena.

They were getting married in the late spring of the coming year. If Dermot came into the office in the dying days of December, he could take a long weekend for the wedding and then a honeymoon to follow. But the reality of Serena spending Christmas Day with her parents and siblings unaccompanied by her boyfriend was a scenario she'd struggled with. Dermot had already received numerous Whatsapp messages, peppered with rolling-eyed emojis at the chaos of food prep and present-opening that was already in full swing at his in-laws' spacious family home in Bearsden. To his shame, he felt relief bloom in his chest as he placed his muted phone in a drawer and logged into the Police Scotland computer system.

*

Dermot was engrossed in proof reading a professional development report on one of the department's new DCs when a knock at the door interrupted his concentration. The cheerful, round face of DC Sharon Moffatt was peering at him through the glass panel of the door. For once, her mass of dirty blonde curls were loose to her shoulders, creating the illusion of a halo around her head.

"Come in!" He called out, with a hint of resignation.

The door swung open as if it had received a hefty shove. Sharon shouldered through it with her arms ladened with plastic containers. "Merry Christmas!"

Dermot watched with interest as his colleague dumped the containers onto the desk, peeled back several lids and tossed him a paper plate. "What's all this?" His eyebrow arched.

"It's Christmas Day. Just because we're on shift, doesn't mean we can't mark the occasion."

Dermot glanced over her shoulder at the rest of the serious crime floor, where half a dozen officers were now seated at their desks and all of them were gripping a plastic cup and stuffing their face with what he assumed were Sharon's offerings.

"I've got cold cuts of ham and turkey, which I cooked last night. In this tin is a game pie which my auntie made."

Dermot smiled, he'd grown used to Sharon's habit of feeding up her workmates. He supposed that at this time of year, the tendency was only likely to escalate. Plus, DS Andy Calder wasn't there to hoover up the majority of the home bakes like he usually was.

To his surprise, the DI felt his stomach grumble. He realised then it was nearly 2pm and he'd had nothing to eat since a double espresso and pastry for breakfast at sunrise. The coffee was from the impressive Italian machine Serena had bought him for his birthday and the pastry slightly stale from a packet.

"I could make up a plate for you?"

Dermot rapidly shook his head. "No, no, that's not necessary. I'll take a slice of that pie and a hunk of the impressively marbled cheese you've got there, please."

"From the farmer's market in my parents' local town," Sharon replied proudly, hacking at it with a disposable knife which was threatening to snap under the strain at any moment.

Dermot received his plateful gratefully. He realised none of his usual preferred eateries would be open today and without this act of unsolicited generosity by his colleague, he wasn't sure when he would have actually eaten again.

"There's my mum's legendary Christmas cake for pud?"

Dermot suppressed a smile. Of course there was. "Maybe later, Sharon. Did you see the message from the DCI?"

"That she's on leave until the 3rd Jan? Yep, and I don't blame her. I can't remember when the boss last had a proper holiday. She said they're heading to the Highlands? Odd choice at this time of year, but certainly pretty." She perched on a chair. "Are you in charge now then?"

Dermot was deflated at the lack of reverence with which the question was delivered. He supposed it was inevitable, he was still only a DI and the new boy to boot. "Yes, the Chief Superintendent asked me to step up last night."

"Well, it's usually a quiet week. It always was in Edinburgh and Lothian, anyways."

Dermot nodded equably. Most of his experience had been in the diplomatic unit. The run-up to Christmas was a busy time for ferrying dignitaries from one embassy party to another. But once it reached the 25th, they all returned to their country houses or flew abroad for the festive season. "I've only known it to be quiet," he agreed.

"Except for the homeless shelters of course," Sharon continued. "This is the busiest period for them. If I'm not on duty, I usually spend a few hours on Christmas day cooking and serving up a hot dinner at a local shelter in the centre of the city."

Dermot stopped chewing his pie and arched a brow. He supposed it made sense. If Sharon was forever feeding him and his colleagues, she was bound to be doing the same for those who actually needed it. "That's a wonderful thing to do. Most cops are desperate for the leave and a bit of peace and quiet."

Sharon shrugged. "The novelty of Christmas day with the parents wears off when you hit about thirty. I prefer Hogmanay, I meet up with friends for a meal and several drams then. I'm no saint," she delivered the final statement with a grin, gathering up her boxes and backing out of the cramped space.

Dermot watched her awkward departure, realising too late he should have held the door for her, or at least carried some of the containers. He shook his head, thinking how a career in public service sometimes made you forget about the little things, the common courtesies that keep the world turning. It too often felt the work they did was above all that. But it really wasn't.

He pulled open the top drawer of the desk and glanced at the screen of his phone. It was full of unread messages from Serena. One contained nothing but a line of angry faced emojis with steam coming out of their ears. Dermot wondered what on earth Serena really had to be so angry about. She was with her loving family, about to be presented with more food than she could ever eat, had a fiancée who endeavoured to give her everything she wished for, including her dream wedding. He quickly shook these disloyal thoughts from his mind and firmly shoved the drawer closed with a metallic clatter.

Chapter 3

The noise of the rotors was deafening when Dani lifted her ear protectors for a moment. She had travelled by helicopter a few times before, but never over snow-capped hills in the middle of winter.

James sat beside her, scanning the landscape below, which was a stunning contrast of black slate against the white covering of recent snowfall. To be fair to her other half, the weather had been kind to them. The wind had died right down and the sky was now a clear blue. The calmness would only last a few hours, but this had been enough for Bernard Raven's chopper to transport them from Edinburgh to the Western Highlands on the morning of Boxing Day.

Dani had hastily packed a case for them both the previous evening, deciding to forego the whisky drinking which had begun in earnest by James and his family after the festive meal had been cleared away and the fire lit.

The DCI didn't have a problem with flying, but a helicopter ride with a whisky hangover wasn't something she wanted to risk. Although, glancing at James now, she could detect no signs of the 'water of life's' ill-effects on him. His face was glowing with a boyish excitement.

Thanks to her boyfriend's warning on Christmas Eve, Dani was able to collect a formal black dress from her flat in Glasgow, a pair of heels and a few pieces of her mother's jewellery to accompany the thick knitted jumpers and jeans which felt like necessary kit for a draughty old castle in December, not to mention the thermal undies she'd bought in

House of Fraser on Buchanan Street and wrapped for them both to place under the Irving's huge tree.

Sally Irving-Bryant had raised an eyebrow as her brother opened the department store box on Christmas morning and modelled the woolly garment over his hound's tooth pyjamas. Sally herself had received a silver and diamond Tiffany pendant from her husband, Grant. Which she informed us was just a little token to open right now, as her real present was a ski trip to St Moritz in the New Year.

Dani didn't begrudge the couple their extravagances. Grant was the CEO of an impressive building company, with active projects the length and breadth of Scotland. In fact, it was James's brother-in-law who had secured him Bernard Raven as a client. The two men's paths had crossed on various occasions. Sally was a top Edinburgh lawyer and was able to be just as generous with her gifts as Grant. They enjoyed having the best of everything, they worked long hours and were often apart in order to obtain it.

Grant was just popping open a bottle of Moët and mixing it with a dash of orange juice for the sake of propriety as James admired his new undergarment. "Very sensible," he'd boomed. "I'd particularly recommend you wear those at night up at Raven's place."

"You've been to his place in Ullapool before?" Dani asked with interest.

"Yes, just the once. I wouldn't say it's in Ullapool exactly. Strathain House is just beyond the Braemore Forest, on the banks of Loch Broom. I think the nearest village is called Inverlael. I stayed there for a weekend to do business with Bernie. Absolutely breath-taking views. The castle isn't too shabby either, there are parts which are medieval, I believe. But I'm sure he'll give you the full tour.

Don't worry, the main building is a sturdy sandstone construction of the gothic revival."

"Does it have central heating?" Dani had shuddered as she asked.

Grant laughed. "Yes, some kind of diesel-fired heating system if I recall, totally off grid, and plenty of open fireplaces that I'm sure he and Morag will have blazing for all you guests at this festive time."

Dani felt marginally more confident. "Is Morag his wife?"

Grant nodded. "Yep, although not his first I seem to remember. Bernie is in his sixties but I'd place Morag as barely fifty. They've got a few staff to run the place, but Morag isn't afraid of rolling her sleeves up. I suspect it's a never-ending battle to keep the place from falling down."

Dani's confidence took a plummet again. "What time of year did you stay?"

Grant rubbed at his reddish stubble. "Och, it must have been around Autumn time because the forests were a beautiful array of oranges and browns. We fished in the loch, where we could look back towards the house and grounds, positioned slightly up the hillside, in a clearing surrounded on all sides by pines."

"So, you needed thermal underwear at night, and it was only Autumn?" Dani's expression became incredulous, her bones already seeming to chill.

James began collecting together discarded paper and moved closer to Dani, wrapping her in his arms, as if she were one of the festive gifts under the tree. "Don't worry darling," he offered. "I'll be there to keep you warm."

"And in case that fails," Grant interrupted loudly, taking a healthy slug of bucks fizz. "I recommend half a bottle of scotch before bed."

Dani smiled at the memory. Peering out of the

concave window by her seat and gasping as a sea of pine forest stretched out beneath them. The undulating mass of snow topped trees and hillsides abruptly parted to reveal the greyish-blue of Loch Broom, glittering under a sharp winter sun.

The pilot's intercom crackled into life and the helicopter tilted as it descended towards the right banks of the loch. Dani held her breath as it appeared they were about to plough into a line of Douglas firs. Then a field of perfectly green grass appeared, as if from nowhere, in stark contrast to the ice and snow sprinkled pines that surrounded it. The chopper put down directly in the centre of the lawn.

The pilot seemed in a hurry as he hauled out their case and bags, pointing towards a gap in the towering trees up ahead. "Head in that direction for the house," he instructed succinctly. "As soon as you're at a safe distance I'm leaving. I've got a window of about two hours before the weather closes in again. I'll be able to get to Inverness by then. Civilisation," he added with a wink which Dani found vaguely disturbing.

The couple carried their luggage in the direction they'd be ordered. They had almost reached the bank of thick tree trunks when they heard the rotor blades start up again.

"Bloody hell, he could've waited until we were well clear," James muttered angrily, his words almost swallowed up by the roar of the chopper's engine.

Dani stopped and turned, instinctively bowing her head as the helicopter raised itself from the ground, turned and flew away over the forest to the south-west. She felt a tightening across her chest. The weather was closing in again in a couple of hours and they'd just watched their only means of transport disappear into the distance.

Here they were in the middle of bloody nowhere with a suitcase and a bottle of single malt. She risked a glance at James, who himself was staring into the rapidly darkening patch of sky which the chopper had recently vacated, with a blank expression on his face.

Chapter 4

The gap in the trees was marked by a pair of stone statues. They were of two classical figures, a man and a woman. Their heads were adorned with a couple of inches of pure white snow. The stone was covered in a light layer of spongey moss, creating a mottled effect which spoke of their age. Dani's education didn't stretch to being able to identify the figures represented.

"It's Adam and Eve, I suspect," James commented, as if he could follow Dani's train of thought. "In the classical style, but most likely Victorian. Grant did say the main house was gothic revival. The Victorians loved all that neo-classical stuff."

"I should have been able to tell who they were. My education wasn't classical, but Dad certainly liked to read us Bible stories in primary school."

"The classical style of sculpture was full of subjects with their kit off, so Adam and Eve were perfect. They also represent a great moral message for the Victorians to peddle, making it a perfect combo for the gothic architects and garden designers."

Dani considered this as they walked along a narrow path amongst the fir trees. The branches were so dense that very little life could flourish on the forest floor beneath. The result was a silence that was eerie. Just the occasional crack of fallen pine needles under their feet broke the hush.

The line of trees must have been carefully planted as they ended abruptly, leaving Dani and James standing on an immaculate lawn which sloped upwards towards the house.

Strathain House sat proudly on the hillside at the end of a long driveway flanked by pristine lawns. The building itself was made with the pinkish sandstone common along the west coast of Scotland. A pair of turrets adorned each end of the house and Dani could barely count the number of leaded windows on the first and second floors.

"It must have dozens of rooms," she gasped.

James pointed. "There you go, a reproduction Roman colonnade to complete the image."

Dani observed the line of stone columns which lay to the east of the main building and seemed to enclose some kind of stone terrace with a pool and water feature. "I'm not sure if it's tacky or beautiful."

There wasn't any time to make a decision one way or the other. The main door to the house had swung open and a tall, broad figure with a whisp of grey hair emerged from it and descended the stone steps towards them. He was dressed in a thick cable-knit jumper the colour of oatmeal which rolled right up to his fleshy chin. Sturdy corduroy trousers completed the casual, lord-of-the-manor look and a black Labrador loitered obediently at his heels.

"James!" The man exclaimed, holding out a large, leathery hand to his guest. "So sorry I didn't come down to meet the chopper. He was half an hour early. Super keen to outrun the weather, apparently."

"Not a problem, Bernard. We found our way perfectly easily." He blew out his cheeks. "This is an amazing place you've got here."

"We like it. I spend all my time designing little modern boxes, I certainly didn't want to be living in one." He turned his surprisingly blue eyes towards Dani. "This must be your partner, Danielle, isn't it?"

"Yes," she replied. "But do please call me Dani."

He nodded with a grin. "Same here, call me Bernie. Neither of us are on duty now."

Dani thought this an odd choice of words. She wondered if James had told the man she was a police officer. But his greeting was quickly forgotten as they entered the entrance hall of Strathain House.

A dark wood carved staircase ascended the wall to the right of them, a galleried landing lay beyond and the walls themselves were adorned with multiple stag heads and ebonised panelling.

"Some find the darkness of the wood oppressive," Bernie said cheerfully. "I should know how popular light, bright interiors are these days, but this hall has floors and panels made by hand from wood which originated in the Braemore Forest itself. 150 years ago, it was all the rage to ebonise everything that moved, which explains the darkness of the finish."

Dani set down her bag on the zig-zagged pattern of the parquet floor. "It's absolutely stunning. A space of this size can withstand a bit of dark wood. It's exactly how you would imagine a Highland castle to look."

Bernie patted her shoulder. "That's exactly the effect we wanted to create. The house was used in the nineteenth century as a hunting lodge for the Badenoch family. They had a primary residence in Colinton in Edinburgh and Robert Badenoch was a financier who made his fortune capitalising on the successes of the Scottish shipping industry. He had Strathain modernised in the 1870s, as a retreat for himself and their growing sons. Some of the medieval structure still exists in places, but most was replaced by solid Caithness sandstone. We try to keep up the hunting and fishing traditions of the place, but I fear Morag and I are city-folk still at heart. We aren't really any good at it."

"When did you buy this place?" James asked politely. Dani sensed he wasn't quite as impressed as she was and had probably seen plenty of similar historic properties in his time.

Bernie indicated they should leave their bags in the hallway and led them through a set of double-doors into a bright sitting room with a bay window facing the drive, with the sweeping waters of the loch beyond. "The house had remained in the Badenoch family until Charles, the grandson of Robert, died four years ago at the age of 102. The place had fallen into complete disrepair. The old man had a handful of staff but there wasn't the money or the inclination to keep the place up. One of my friends in the construction industry mentioned it to me, thought I may want to turn it into a hotel, or luxury flats."

Their host approached a large open fireplace, bending down to pick up a log from a full basket and tossing it onto the embers crackling in the grate. The Labrador dropped down heavily onto the oriental rug placed in front of the fender.

"In fact," Bernie continued, "I fell in love with it. Morag and I weren't long married and I felt I wanted a proper home for us both. So I put in a ridiculously low offer which was accepted rather too enthusiastically." He smiled ruefully. "The agent knew just how many issues the old place had."

"You and Morag have renovated the place?" Dani couldn't keep the awe out of her voice.

"Well, I have extensive building contacts and an excellent team myself, so if anyone was going to take on such a project, it had to be someone like me."

Dani turned her head towards another door leading out of the sitting room to their right. She had heard the sound of heels clipping across the parquet. Seconds later, a willowy woman with dark, shoulder-length hair and what looked like Laboutin shoes paired with skinny Levi's and a silk blouse entered the room.

"Ah, Morag, I was just regaling our guests with the story of this old place."

Morag gave a tinkle of a laugh. "I expect they haven't even had a chance to freshen up after their journey yet! Have you even been offered a pot of tea?"

Dani smiled. "We were getting the tour first. It's a wonderful house." Her admiration was genuine so she hoped it came across that way.

"It is wonderful, but also an old tyrant. We pulled down rotten panels and found damp and dry-rot everywhere. For what we've spent on this place we could be living on the waterfront in LA."

Bernie tutted loudly. "And where would be the fun in that, eh? Too many people for starters, everyone living on top of one another and no privacy." He visibly shuddered.

"Ah, but think of all that sunshine," Morag added playfully, she turned to James and Dani. "Don't worry, your room has a large radiator and the sun in the mornings. We may very well have a thick covering of snow by tonight, which acts as a wonderful insulator."

Dani was impressed by her optimism. Morag wore nothing but a flimsy blouse but seemed unaffected by the chill which was felt anywhere outside the direct proximity of the fireplace. The detective also tried to place the woman's accent, which was a more refined Scots than her husband's coarser dialect.

Bernie abruptly reached for a brass bell hanging by the fire surround and rang it with some force. Dani hadn't thought anyone actually summoned their staff in such a manner outside of Downton Abbey. She gave James a sideward glance and raised an eyebrow archly.

"It's time we had some refreshments," Bernie boomed. "And you can meet a few of your fellow guests."

Chapter 5

The dining room table had already been set. Dani ran her hand along the smooth, chestnut coloured wood, deciding it was pure mahogany and very likely an antique. A china tea-set sat on a tray and an assortment of cakes and sandwiches were placed on glass stands within easy reach of the guests.

All of the principal reception rooms seemed to face the front of the house, with a view of the loch. The kitchens, she assumed, were at the rear. Three couples in addition to Dani and James were seated around the table, although there was room for at least six more people. Bernie and Morag had left them to it, gone to help prepare their rooms perhaps?

The middle-aged man seated in front of Dani with a thick salt and pepper beard and a tweed suit complete with waistcoat leant forward to pour tea into her cup.

"Yes please," she commented. "It may help to warm me up."

"You've travelled up from the south, then?" He ventured.

"Well, from Edinburgh today, but we live in Glasgow."

He nodded knowingly. "I'm Allan Baxter, this is my wife, Helen." He indicated the neat, strongly built woman beside him with a sculpted bob of ash-blonde hair, stirring sugar into her tea. "We live in Inverlael, the town just about five miles north along the loch. I run a veterinary practice in the town. I've got to know Bernie tending to his cattle. He's got a couple of grazing pastures up the glen."

Dani introduced herself and James. She stressed her boyfriend's connection to the Ravens, unwilling to talk about herself too much. She was here as James's partner, and police talk tended to bring down even the liveliest social gathering.

A tall red-head further down the table got to her feet, stretching over to cut a slice from one of the impressive cakes that Dani was sure must have been brought in from outside by caterers. Morag hadn't struck her as the baking type. This woman, in her mid-thirties, Dani assessed, turned shyly to her fellow guests, making eye contact with each one. 'Please help yourselves to the cakes, they will only be fresh today. Morag ordered them from a gorgeous new artisan bakery in Ullapool. She and Bernie send their apologies for not being here to welcome you all just yet, they've got some business to attend to before the celebrations can begin in earnest." She smiled broadly, revealing a neat set of white teeth with an endearing gap at the centre of the top row.

The man seated beside her, of a similar age but with a receding hairline that at first glance made him look older, cleared his throat theatrically behind his fist.

The woman laughed slightly nervously. "Sorry, I meant to introduce myself. I'm Sasha Preston and this is my husband, Oliver. Bernie is my uncle. He invited me and Oli up for the big party, we live in Manchester. Travelled up a few days ago when the weather was better." Her nervous giggle exploded forth once again.

Dani smiled kindly, "James here is a work colleague of Bernard's. We are visiting from Glasgow. You mentioned a big party, do you mean Hogmanay?" Dani's mind drifted to the simple and uninspiring black slip dress she'd brought with her. She hoped it wouldn't be a black tie event.

A hand flew up to Sasha Preston's crimson painted mouth, "Oh, did I? I just meant the house party, you know, celebrating the festive season and all that." She sat down heavily on her chair, looking as if she felt she'd said something she shouldn't.

The final couple had remained silent during this time, sipping tea and observing them all over the rim of their delicate china cups. It was Allan Baxter who brought them into the discussion. "And how do you know the Ravens? Are you staying until the New Year?"

It was the man who answered. He was small and wizened, in a grey suit that would have made him look like a school boy from a distance. His accent was a sing-song Irish burr, "Oh we've travelled a long way to be here this week. Dorothy and I caught the boat to Holyhead and made our way from there. We wouldn't have come such a long distance if we weren't staying," he put in matter-of-factly. "We are the Shannahans, Dorothy and Anthony."

The rest of the group muttered their greetings. Dani observed Dorothy Shannahan sitting absolutely still in the high-backed chair. She was an apple-shaped woman who was no taller than her husband. Her mouth had barely formed so much as a flicker of a smile since they'd arrived at the table. Dani sensed this was a couple well outside their comfort zone. She thought perhaps they were Tony and Dot to their friends and family back home in Ireland, but here in this grand castle amongst strangers, they were giving nothing away.

It was Helen Baxter, a well-built and practical looking woman who pushed back her chair and laid a linen napkin on the table. "Well, that was very pleasant, but I think it's about time Allan and I went up to our room to unpack. To be honest, I'm starting to pick up a wee chill in this room." She cast her eye to the bay window, which despite a heavy set of drapes adorning each corner, was emitting a noticeable draught of ice cold air.

Dani looked beyond to the scene outside. The tiny sprinkling of snow that had begun when they arrived had morphed into huge flakes which were settling on the lawn at a rapid pace. The path which ran down the centre was no longer visible. She couldn't help but shiver.

"Oh no!" Sasha exclaimed. "We are supposed to wait here until Morag informs us that our rooms are ready. The housekeeper is seeing to them. I don't even know where everyone is sleeping yet." Her husband laid a soothing hand on her arm. He seemed to be a master of non-verbal communication.

James moved across to the fireplace, where the embers were low. He looked around for logs, locating a basket just inside the club fender. He picked a couple up and tossed them onto the grate. With several firm jabs of the iron poker, the flames once again sprung to life. "Come and gather around here, Helen. It's much warmer than over by the bay. In these big old places it's about finding the comfortable spots. There's no chance of heating the whole castle."

Helen shrugged her broad shoulders and strode towards the fireplace. James pulled out a high-backed Queen Anne style armchair for her. "These chairs were designed in the 18th Century. The high backs are to keep out the draughts for the days before central heating."

"I thought this place was supposed to have central heating," Dani added dryly.

Allan had moved across to join them. "The same principle applies to the old wicker lambing chairs that were crafted up in the Orkney Islands. The backs are high and the seats low, so that the farmer can stay up all night to milk the wee lambs and keep the cold out. I've got several clients around here who still have them out in their barns."

Dorothy Shannahan shifted in her seat, letting out a small sigh. She clearly wasn't interested in the history of Highland furniture. Her husband glanced at her with concern. "Do we have any idea how long Bernie and Morag might be?" Tony addressed the question to Sasha, who seemed to have established herself as their hosts' spokesperson.

Sasha's brow creased with worry, she had clearly wanted to make her speech and retire into the background. "I honestly don't know. Morag just said to wait here for them."

"Why don't you give Morag a call?" Dani gently suggested.

The younger woman's brow knitted even more tightly together, giving an indication of where the lines would be in a decade's time. "There's no mobile signal on this side of the loch." The words were spoken faintly, as if she hoped they'd not be heard properly.

James stepped towards the table. "Hang on. You mean we can't make any calls on our mobiles from the house? What about Wi-Fi? I'm pretty sure I've got Bernie on a Whatsapp group?"

Sasha's expression was stricken, as if she was under interrogation by officers of some totalitarian state. Her husband intervened. "Look, we don't know much more than you except we arrived a few days earlier. Our room is on the second floor, facing towards the forest. I assume all the guests must be staying along that corridor, it doesn't seem as if the upper floors are properly refurbished." He leant forward, resting his elbows on the polished mahogany. "I drove into Inverlael yesterday and picked up some 4G to call my office. But as far as I can tell, there's no signal here on the estate. Although Bernie certainly has a landline telephone."

Dani gazed out of the window at the grey sky and steady fall of snowflakes. The green of the immaculate lawns had been replaced by a deep blanket of pure white. "So we have to drive into town in order to go onto the Internet?" She swiped the screen of her phone, perhaps in the vague hope that it was somehow an exception. The top line of the home screen was an unfamiliar blank. "But look at the weather. That's not going to be so easy, is it?"

Sasha's expression brightened at this. "Oh, Uncle Bernie's got a Land Rover. He can take you in and out, no trouble!"

James didn't feel overly reassured by this suggestion. Although he was on leave from his solicitors firm, he never left himself unreachable. Then there was his mother, who wasn't in the greatest of health. Despite the chill of the vast dining room, James felt sweat begin to prickle under his collar.

It was Helen Baxter who expressed the frustration they were all beginning to feel. "Well, this isn't acceptable," she boomed. "We've left Andy at home with the dogs for the week. He's 17 and perfectly capable, but as I'm sure you'll understand, we do need to be in regular contact with him. I message him every few hours. Our son doesn't know what a *landline* is, for heaven's sake!"

Dani was about to suggest that if this was the case the Baxters should return to their house in Inverlael before the weather worsened, when a familiar click-clack of heels approached the double-doors of the dining room.

Morag Raven emerged from the shadows with a beaming smile on her face. "Getting to know one another better I do hope!" She declared. "Now, I'll call Mrs Noble in to clear away the tea things and you can follow me up to the second floor where your accommodation will be. I do hope you love the rooms, I can't wait to show you all what we've done with them."

If one of the group had wanted to ask about the lack of internet access or phone reception, Morag's entrance seemed to have silenced them. Each couple fell into a line behind their hostess, obediently allowing her to lead them towards the snaking oak staircase and the floor above.

Chapter 6

The double room that Dani and James had been given was certainly impressive. They didn't have a view of the loch through the large sash windows, but of the forest to the south-west which had created a dense, green canopy over the hillside. There was a silvery sheen of snow across the very tops of the trees. But the branches of the firs were so compactly interwoven that the ground underneath was clear of ice and snow.

Rather than the dark wood interiors of the ground floor reception areas, this room had been furnished with lightly sanded pine and elder. The linen was ivory and the en-suite newly fitted with a honey-coloured marble sink and bath.

The winter sun was spilling through the window and a modern radiator sat on one of the walls, pumping out enough heat to compel Dani to pull off her woollen sweater.

"What do you think of the room?" James asked warily, sinking into the thick mattress beside her.

"I think this room is absolutely gorgeous, but I also know I am a senior police officer who cannot be out of reach of Pitt Street, no matter where I happen to be on holiday."

James grimaced. "I know, I can't be out of the loop with my office either, although I know it's not as life or death as it is for you. I had no idea this place was so cut off." He lowered his voice. "If Bernie had told me, I would never have asked you to come, I swear."

Dani sighed. "I know you wouldn't. Being in contact with your mum is so important to you, I completely understand that." She threw up her hands in defeat. "Morag let me use the phone in Bernie's office. I've left their number with Dermot at Pitt Street and with your dad. That should be sufficient. We did live quite happily once without mobile phones and the internet, you know."

James slipped his arms around her waist, resting his head on her shoulder. "Yes, I remember it well. When I was at boarding school we got one phone call home a week. Other than that it was letters. Mum and Dad have kept all the ones I wrote them, tied up in a box somewhere."

Dani touched her lips to the top of his head. "I can't quite imagine DCS Douglas sending me a postcard if he needs to get in touch."

James's body rocked with a deep chuckle. "No, I certainly can't either." He lifted his head and placed a kiss on her lips. "Still need warming up?"

"Actually, it's just about the right temperature in here." She breathed in his smell; of wood smoke from the fire he had revived in the dining room and a vague hint of aviation fuel from the chopper. His lips, though, tasted of tea and icing sugar.

James nuzzled her neck, tugging at the seam of her thermal vest. "Perhaps if you removed a few layers, you'd be more comfortable?"

Dani was about to lift the vest over her head when she stopped dead. Her attention had been drawn by a movement on the floor near the door of their room. She pulled away from James's cosy embrace.

"Hey, what's up?" He ruffled his hair in frustration.

The area was in shadow, away from the beams of sun slicing through the leaded window panes and criss-crossing the four-poster bed. Dani crouched on her hands and knees, feeling along the uneven floorboards until her fingers rested on the surface of a smooth piece of paper, folded in two. "Someone just pushed this under our door," she said quietly, before rising to standing height and dragging the heavy, panelled door open.

Dani stepped out into the corridor in her thick socks. There was nobody there. All the other identical doors were closed. She retreated inside, pushing the door shut behind her and instinctively turning the key in the lock.

"What does it say?" James was just in front of her, his expression only mildly concerned. "Maybe one of us has had a phone message?"

Dani shrugged, thinking it would be a very odd way of communicating the information if so, unless a member of staff heard their lowered, intimate voices through the panelling and decided they wouldn't want to be disturbed. She dismissed this idea and opened out the sheet of writing paper, which was substantial and evidently expensive. Inside was written, in black ink and block capitals:

"WHY ARE YOU HERE?".

She handed it to James, all too aware that in her professional life, this note would be placed immediately in an evidence bag where it could no longer pick up further fingerprints or have the microscopic evidence which existed on its delicate surface smudged by over handling.

In this place, so remote and insulated by the thick covering of Highland snow and encircled by dense forest and the deep loch, so far from the forensic labs of Pitt Street, the note didn't seem much worth preserving.

James placed the note on the bed. "What do you think it means? Is the question meant for you, or me?"

Dani shook her head. "I've got no idea. I went with Morag into Bernie's office earlier, it was full of ink pens and quality stationery like this."

"Well it could hardly be Bernie or Morag asking why we are here. They're the ones who bloody invited us!"

"Yes, I just meant that Bernie's office is perfectly accessible to anyone who might have wanted to write the note. The Baxters went in there after me to call their son for a start."

James sighed. "I can't see why the local vet would have any particular interest in our presence here, nor that quiet Irish couple. Bernie's niece seemed pleased to welcome us all to the castle in her uncle's absence. I didn't sense any resentment at having to share the place with the rest of us."

Dani frowned. She agreed with James, the note didn't seem to make any sense at all. The Shannahans had been quiet and uncomfortable in the company of their fellow guests, but they gave off the distinct impression they were struggling to understand what *they* were doing at Strathain House, let alone anyone else.

"Maybe it's a mistake," James added brightly. "It's not addressed to anybody. All the doors on this corridor look exactly the same. It could be meant for someone else. It certainly doesn't mean anything to us, does it?"

"No, it doesn't." Dani was mulling over the words.

James picked up the note again and placed it in a drawer in the dresser under the window, sliding it firmly shut. He moved towards Dani and took her hands. "Let's forget about it. The message was fairly cryptic and could have been directed at any of the guests here. I'm pretty sure Morag and Bernie have an amazing meal planned for tonight. I'll get that bottle of single malt out of the case and we can open it after dinner. What do you think?"

Dani managed a smile. "Yes, that sounds like a plan. I was too intrigued by this old place and our fellow guests to have eaten much at afternoon tea, I'm actually starving."

James pulled her into a chaste embrace, the previous romantic atmosphere dispelled by the odd message. Dani relaxed into his arms, but her mind was still ticking over. She was thinking about the disparate group the Ravens had invited to this castle for the festive season. None of them appeared to have much in common, or seemed likely to hit it off as firm friends. They were certainly an odd bunch. James had only worked on one deal with Bernie and had barely known the man more than six months. It certainly wasn't an acquaintanceship worthy of a week's stay over Christmas.

Dani pictured the note sitting in the empty drawer, suddenly feeling that the question posed within it wasn't a bad one. Just what exactly were her and James doing here?

Chapter 7

The reception desk had received a call at 6pm on Boxing Day. It had been put through to Sharon's extension soon after. One of the townhouses in a modern development on Clyde Wharf had been broken into. The alarm had gone off, but it had taken over an hour for anyone to call the police. The security firm that fitted the alarm system were understaffed over the Christmas period.

Dermot drove his BMW estate through the open gates and into the small but secluded courtyard entrance to the development. He noted the slush had been shovelled away to form a series of grey mounds at the edges of the quad. "We promise you 24/7 protection for your home, except over Christmas when we'll be at home face-stuffing mince-pies."

Sharon laughed. "Those house alarms are always going off. People have learnt to ignore it and when that happens, the burglars get busy."

They climbed out of the car and approached the front door that had a crime tape draped across it and had been propped open with a brick.

"Squad car got here ahead of us," Sharon said by way of explanation.

Dermot examined the door, which was solid composite wood, no window pane. "Doesn't look as if the front door was the entry point." He reached into his pocket for a pair of sky blue evidence gloves, noticing Sharon was already wearing hers.

The ground floor of the property housed a modern kitchen area and a door which Dermot knew led to the carport. It was one of those properties where the living room and bedrooms were on the upper two floors to take advantage of the views, which in this case was a fairly uninspiring section of the Clyde still very much in the process of redevelopment.

A quick glance at the kitchen revealed a window swinging open above the sink. The aperture faced out onto a tiny paved courtyard. Iron railings provided a barrier to a narrow dirt path that ran along the banks of the river beyond.

"We've found the entry point," Dermot said levelly. "This is where the forensic team will need to thoroughly dust for fingerprints." He glanced down into the sparkling chrome sink, hoping to see a few drops of blood, perhaps from the intruder cutting themselves on broken glass, or snagging an arm on the iron spikes. No such luck, the surface was clean. The burglar must have jumped straight over the top.

Sharon was making notes on her phone as they moved through the house. Obviously following his train of thought, she added, "the intruder must be fit and nimble to get through that narrow window and leapfrog the worktop."

"Yep," Dermot agreed. "They must have deliberately avoided the front entrance. There's no way past the gate without a code for starters and a CCTV camera pointed at your face."

Sharon stretched on her toes to peer out of the window. "The rear of the properties, on the other hand, leads to an isolated path running alongside the Clyde at one of its least salubrious stretches."

"I believe the area is referred to as, 'up and coming'." Dermot raised an eyebrow.

They climbed the dark staircase which led to the first floor, comprising a living room with balcony and two of the four bedrooms. A PC was surveying the mess the burglar had left in his wake; books strewn about the floor, tables upturned, the sofa pushed out into the centre of the space.

"DI Muir and DS Moffat. Thanks for getting here so swiftly." Dermot flashed his warrant card.

The PC stepped carefully over the debris. "No problem, Sir. We were on patrol a couple of miles away when the call came in. It'd been fairly quiet before that. My colleague is upstairs checking the master suite. It looks like some cash and jewellery are gone, maybe some tech devices, but until we check with the owners we can't be sure."

"They left the TV?" Dermot dipped his head towards the 60 inch screen suspended from the wall opposite them.

"Whoever broke in wasn't going to get that thing out through the window downstairs, Sir. They must have been looking for whatever they could walk out with, opportunist maybe?" The young PC offered.

Sharon walked up to the huge slimline television and tugged at it with some force, it didn't budge. "It's well secured to the wall there. At least the owner knows how to attach a decent wall bracket. If it's difficult to remove from a premises, a burglar will leave it behind. Always bracket your expensive TV," she added with a wink.

Dermot thought about the wide screen TV Serena had chosen for their flat. It was currently placed on a faux marble coffee table by the window, whilst he was at work over Christmas and she was staying at her parents' house. They should really take more care with the expensive items Serena liked to collect around her. Perhaps his relaxed attitude to home security suggested how little these things meant to him. His fiancé's throwaway attitude was more difficult to explain.

The PC glanced at his notebook. "The owners are called Fleetwood. They are spending Christmas and

New Year in Tenerife, this is according to one of the neighbours. They hadn't informed their security company of this fact, which is why they hadn't got the property on an alert, a common practice when a client tells them they're on holiday."

"That helps explain the late response to the alarm going off," Sharon sighed. "Why go to the trouble of spending a small fortune and then not bothering to inform your home security firm when your expensive property is going to be empty?" She exaggeratedly rolled her eyes, making the PC crack a smile.

Dermot was about to ask the junior officer to wait for forensics, then arrange for the broken window to be secured for the night when a shout came from the floor above.

"That's Kev," the PC said with concern. "What the hell's going on?"

Dermot put his arm out to prevent the PC from bolting up the stairs ahead of him. Instead, he stalked up the narrow stairwell first, his hand running along the smooth painted wall, wishing he at least had his baton with him.

It was quiet when Dermot reached the landing on the third floor. He swung left, assuming the master bedroom would be the one facing the river. He was right. A pair of patio doors stood open to a tiny balcony, ice-cold December air hit him like a slap to the face.

A uniformed officer he assumed to be Kev, was standing with his legs apart on the balcony, gripping the jacket of a young lad, perhaps just a teenager, who was trying to launch himself over the iron railings, a bulky object tucked under one armpit.

The pair hadn't yet seen him. Dermot took three strides forward, grateful for the cushioning of the thick pile carpet which muffled each step. Kev had sensed his approach and gave him an almost imperceptible nod of the head.

Dermot launched forwards, seizing the fleeing boy around the waist. At the same moment, Kev wrenched the jacket backwards. All three collapsed unceremoniously through the open patio doors, landing with a thump, the object clattering down softly on the plush carpet Dermot found he was once again enormously grateful for.

Chapter 8

By the time they were summoned to the library for pre-dinner drinks, it was dark as pitch outside. Dani stared out of the bedroom window, trying to tell if it was still snowing. She couldn't decide.

James had changed his shirt and had a shave. He pulled the bottle of scotch out of their case. "I'm ready for a glass of this and it's not even 7 o'clock yet."

Dani wore a red blouse with a high collar, but had refused to change out of her jeans. She knew it would be chilly downstairs and her desire to play the perfect houseguest was seriously on the wane. She thought about the odd group assembled beneath them. "I think hitting the bottle is going to be the only way to survive this."

James grinned stoically. "Come on, detective, let's get this over with."

The library of Strathain House was a delightful room. A fire raged in the hearth and the walls were lined with oak shelving filled with leather-bound spines. A nine foot Douglas Fir stood in a pot within the bay recess and was decorated tastefully with glass baubles, brass bells and tinsel which reflected the glow of the dancing flames.

A woman who Dani placed in her sixties was delivering drinks to them with a fixed smile. She wore a navy blue wrap dress and low heels. Dani assumed she was the housekeeper.

Bernie and Allan Baxter stood by the fireplace, both holding a tumbler of Whisky Sour. They were discussing the health of Bernie's herd of Highland Cattle.

James and Dani had opted for an 'Old Fashioned'. As had Helen Baxter and Tony Shannahan. Morag was addressing their group, gripping a glass with a profusion of green sprigs poking out above the rim. "You should really try a 'Mint Julep' next, they're all the rage in the States. Of course, they add bourbon to it over there, rather than single malt, which is blasphemy to us." Her laugh was like the tinkling of the brass bells hanging from the tree beside them.

Dani smiled politely, turning to Tony. "Is your wife not joining us?"

He cleared his throat. "Dorothy has picked up a chill from our boat crossing, she'll not be down tonight."

"Mrs Noble is taking her up a bowl of soup and some sandwiches," Morag added in a sympathetic tone.

"I spoke to Andy earlier," Helen interjected. "It turns out he does actually know how to pick up a telephone receiver. Who knew?" Her dark brows arched. "He says the roads into Inverlael are impassable. They've had ten inches of snow fall in the last few hours, with more forecast for tomorrow. I don't think we could return home if we tried."

Morag's expression was serious. "Yes, our groundsman, Pete, is doing his best to clear the driveways. He lives in the lodge on the edge of the forest. Even in the Land Rover, nobody can get far."

"What about supplies? It sounds like we're completely cut off!" Tony's voice was high-pitched and panicky.

Morag laid a perfectly manicured hand on his arm. "We were fully stocked up for your visit here. Mrs Noble has three industrial freezers and a pantry you could get lost in."

Dani thought that was all well and good, as long as they had power. "Do you have your own generator here?"

Morag's mouth tightened a fraction, as if mildly irritated by the question. "The estate covers 12 acres, Dani, including a herd of Highlands, we couldn't survive without an independent power supply. Our generator is in one of the barns. It's diesel-powered, but we are also experimenting with solar panels."

Dani nodded, realising she was supposed to be impressed. To be fair, it did reassure her that they still had access to power if the grid went down, which in these conditions, it invariably did. But again, it all depended on how much diesel they had in that barn.

James drained his old-fashioned, allowing his gaze to travel along the rows of books. "I'd love to have a library like this. I'd happily stay in here for hours."

"Bernie loves that leather armchair over there. The arms are worn down to the wood. He sits in here with a book and a whisky most evenings." Morag gave a start as out in the hallway, the dog began barking ferociously.

Bernie strode out of the room. "Jet! What on earth has got into you, boy? I haven't heard you bark since you were a puppy!"

The group couldn't help but gravitate to join him, wondering what the furore was about. The old black Labrador was standing at the foot of the stairs, its tail ram-rod straight like a weather vane, barking up at Sasha and Oliver, who were standing, frozen, on the middle landing.

Bernie grabbed the dog by its collar. "Come with me, you silly old thing," he chided affectionately. "You can sit with Mrs N in the kitchen."

With the canine threat removed, the younger couple made their way unsteadily down the final few treads to join the others. Morag rushed forward. "I'm terribly sorry, Sasha. Jet doesn't usually do that. Something must have spooked him. He really is a harmless old thing."

From the look of Sasha's bloodless features, she wasn't entirely convinced. Oliver was holding her hand so tightly his knuckles were white.

"The answer to this is a stiff drink," Allan suggested cheerfully. "I'll go and get Mrs Noble to fix you one. We're having Whisky cocktails, I'll tell her to surprise you." He blustered off in the direction of his friend.

Helen stepped forward and took Sasha's other arm, leading her firmly towards the library. "Come in here and take a seat by the fire."

When Sasha was settled, a little colour had returned to her cheeks. She wore a long bohemian style dress that flattered her tall figure and showed off her flame-red tresses. Helen patted her hand. "Allan and I love animals almost more than humans, but they are unpredictable. They can love the people you think least deserving of their adoration and take against those tipped for sainthood. In one respect they are all the same; show them some attention, offer them a treat and a gentle hand and all will be forgotten."

Sasha smiled thinly. "Yes, I'm sure you're right. I have seen Jet before and he certainly didn't react that way to us. But then, I'm not used to dogs at all. Oliver and I are city people really."

"Well, I wouldn't make too much of it," Morag said breezily, "Jet's probably going a bit doolally in his dotage. Here's Allan with your drinks. We'd best take
them through to the dining room. Mrs Noble will be serving dinner soon."

Chapter 9

The young man was seated in an interview room with the duty solicitor, his head hanging down and a quiff of damp hair obscuring his face.

Sharon exited into the corridor, closed the door gently and addressed her senior officer. "Has he spoken yet?"

"Not a word," Dermot replied gruffly.

"Then we don't know how old he is?"

"I asked June on the reception desk to take a look at him as we led him in, she's got teenage boys. According to her, he's young. No more than fourteen."

Sharon whistled. "Too young for us to interview without a parent, then. I'd better get onto Child Protection. There's probably a gang out there who sent him in that window to steal the goods. There's no sign of the rest of the stolen property, only the Xbox console he had gripped in his hands when you and Kevin Planter brought him down off that railing. So he must have handed the rest to them and they made off with it, leaving the poor lad to face the music."

"The MO sounds like County Lines, but then the boy would be a drug addict, doing their bidding for his next high. Somehow, this kid doesn't seem like he's on anything. He's well built, nicely dressed, strong, his pupils weren't dilated." Dermot shrugged. "But hell, I'm no expert."

"There must be a family somewhere missing him. It's *Boxing Day* for heaven's sake."

"Sadly, we know only too well there are plenty of parents who wouldn't give a crap about that. Especially if he's a lad who's gone off the rails and got into drugs."

"But you don't think he has?" Sharon said curiously.

"It's just a hunch, really. He was clinging on so tightly to that Xbox. Maybe he wanted to sell it for drugs, but it felt more like he was trying to protect the thing, like it was a pet or something. If he'd tried to climb down the balcony without it, he could have reached the one below and had a much better chance of escape."

"The console has been taken off to forensics to dust for prints. Do you think we'll find a match on the database?"

Dermot sighed heavily. "There's no way a kid of his age will have his prints on the database. It would have required parental consent and a criminal charge."

Sharon glanced back at the closed door. "The boy doesn't seem to be causing any problems right now. I can call Child Protection, but what are the chances of them sending out a member of the team at 11pm on Boxing Day night?"

"The boy isn't in any current danger, or in need of medical assistance, so that would be about zero."

"Correct. So why don't we send the duty solicitor home to her nearest and dearest for the remainder of the festive season and bring him up to the family room. It's warm up there and I might just have some of my Christmas cake left."

Dermot's eyes sparkled with amusement. "And our teenage tearaway might just have his tongue loosened by some booze-soaked fruit cake with marzipan icing?"

Sharon gave him a wink. "My thoughts precisely."

Chapter 10

The family room was almost unpleasantly warm. A corner sofa and matching armchairs squared off a section of the room. A small kitchenette filled the rest of the space. Sharon busied herself pouring water in the kettle and opening and closing cupboard doors, pulling out jars and checking the best before dates. "How about a hot chocolate?" She threw the suggestion over her shoulder.

The boy was sitting on the edge of the sofa, long arms wrapped around his body and his legs tucked up beneath him. He shrugged, keeping his gaze firmly trained on the threadbare carpet.

Sharon glanced over. "Sorry, didn't catch that. I don't speak 'teenager'. We may need to wait for an interpreter before refreshments can be accurately dispensed." She had no idea if imperious sarcasm would be a wise approach in this situation, but it often worked with her niece and nephew.

He let out a frustrated sigh. "Actually, I'd rather have a coffee."

His accent was definitely Glasgow, but not the thick brogue of a working class lad from the southside. Sharon tossed out a few sachets onto the worktop. "Well, I can only offer you instant. Personally, I avoid the coffee in this place. It's better to buy your own in from *Joseph's* round the corner. What's your usual tipple, flat white, Americano?"

"Double espresso with frothed milk, one sugar." he mumbled into his lap.

Sharon couldn't help releasing a boom of a laugh. "What ya' laughin' at?!" He exclaimed with indignation.

God, these teenagers were so easy to wind up, so earnest and full of woe. "You just get a different class of child criminal in Glasgow these days."

He finally raised his head and met her eyes. "Are you supposed to speak like that to me? In fact, I don't think you're meant to talk to me at all without ma folks here."

"I was only offering you a drink." Sharon made a milky coffee and placed a slice of cake on a paper plate, carrying them over and placing them on the low table.

"Ta," he mumbled, seeming to be desperate not to accept the offerings but suddenly grabbing the slice of cake and stuffing half of it into his mouth.

"You must be hungry, eh?. You've been at the station three hours already. How long before that did you last eat?"

He washed down the fruitcake with a gulp of coffee, wiping his lips with the back of his hand. "I had breakfast."

"I'll send out for some proper food soon. There must be a few take-outs open in Glasgow on Boxing Day. What's your junk food of choice? KFC? Macky D's?" She dipped her head towards the paper plate, now covered in a scattering of crumbs. "Deep-fried Christmas cake?"

This time his lips quivered into a half smile. "You're bonkers. Are you really a cop?"

"Yep, they can't get anyone sane to do the job these days, especially over Christmas. Only nutcases aren't at home with their family from the 25th-26th December. It's official." She saw a glimmer of emotion flicker across his greenish eyes, hurt perhaps, even anger? "I'm a bit old to be with my mum and dad, though they'd still love me to be. I haven't got a husband and kids. So, why aren't you with your family?"

His head dropped forward again. A size 8 foot with a black and white Nike trainer on was unfolded and started to nervously kick the leg of the table.

Sharon waited it out, sipping her tea. It was going to be a long, quiet shift. The snow had stopped falling but the centre of Glasgow was a slushy mess. Anyone with any sense was at home watching rubbish TV, eating leftovers. There was nowhere else for her to be.

He clasped his hands around the mug, as if for comfort. "My favourite is KFC. That's what I had yesterday, for Christmas dinner."

Sharon's stomach lurched. She wasn't often affected by the hard luck stories they heard in the job, you wouldn't last five minutes if you let yourself. But this piece of information made tears prickle at her eyes. She cleared her throat. "Were you with the others? The ones who sent you into that house?"

His head swung up again, a look of pure confusion on his face, which Sharon could now see had a red sprinkling of acne across each cheek. "What are you talking about?"

"Well, there's no way you planned that burglary on your own. For starters, they would have needed a specialist wrench to get that window open and the jewellery that was missing from the box in the bedroom, you didn't have it on you when you were making your escape. So where is it?"

He shook his head of floppy hair, eyeing Sharon like she was one sandwich short of a picnic. "*I* wasn't the one who was burgling the place!"

"But you were climbing over the balcony with an Xbox under your arm when two officers apprehended you. Who else are you claiming to be? Father Christmas in reverse?"

His face flushed crimson as realisation dawned. "That's why you're questioning me! Because you think I'm a bloody burglar, part of some gang!" The coffee had spilt onto the table top, his hands were now shaking so violently. "The Xbox is *mine*. I got it for Christmas. I was *protecting* it. I wasn't burgling the house, I can't have been, I sodding *live* there!"

Chapter 11

The vast house was in silence except for the occasional hoot of an owl outside. Dani imagined the birds nesting on rafters in one of the old barns, keeping out of the cold, snowy night.

When they returned to their rooms, at just before midnight, a couple of hot water bottles with jolly tartan covers had been left on their bed. Dani got the hint and filled both from the mini-kettle on the side table.

As the hours ticked by, the heat from the bottles had gradually diminished, so that Dani could now feel the chill beginning to creep beneath the covers where she and James were intertwined to conserve warmth.

James's breathing was a low rumble, indicating he was fast asleep after enjoying a rich meal and several tumblers of single malt, not to mention the cocktails. Dani had not found it so easy to settle.

After the incident with Jet, Sasha and Oliver Preston had spent the evening meal clearly on edge. Tony Shannahan barely uttered a word to the group, speaking only to his immediate neighbours and only if addressed. He retired to check on his wife the minute the dessert course was over.

It was the Baxters who seemed most at home in the situation. It seemed clear they dined regularly with Morag and Bernie. She supposed it made sense, them living in the nearby town and Allan obviously travelling out to tend to the cattle on a regular basis.

At least Dani had discerned the relationship between Bernie and the Shannahans. She was seated next to Tony at the table. After probing him about children (they have two, now grown up and moved away) Dani asked how he knew the Ravens.

Tony was picking at his poached salmon, pushing sprigs of samphire around the plate. "We worked together, a long time ago. Before Bernie became the big boss."

"What did you do?"

"Manufacturing. Not far out of Glasgow. Most of us didn't get much beyond the production line, but Bernie always had something about him, a spark of unpredictability. He switched to the building trade when our business went into decline. I worked on renovation projects for him over the following years, my restoration skills and carpentry are pretty good. Then I retired with Dotty back to Ireland."

Dani nodded, happy to have got so much information out of the man, who seemed naturally taciturn. She imagined it was the two old-fashioneds he'd already sunk.

"We go way back," Tony continued, his voice lowering a notch. "I knew his first wife. I suppose that's why I've been invited. There aren't many of us left of the old gang. Dotty didn't want to come. She doesn't travel much these days, but then she couldn't let me come alone either, so that was that."

Dani wondered why Dotty couldn't allow Tony to come here on his own, or why they couldn't just have cancelled. It wouldn't have been unusual given the time of year and the weather, the excuses not to attend such a gathering were plentiful.

She glanced over at James's sleeping form. Her boyfriend had given no excuses not to come to this house party, keen to keep on Bernie's good side, to cement him as a client. But did that really explain why they'd abandoned their families at the last minute to travel here at Christmas, with the type of weather even Bear Grylls would hesitate to battle?

Despite the hot water bottles now being stone-cold, the bed suddenly felt oppressive to Dani, the sheets pinning her down and constricting her chest, not allowing her to breathe. She slid her legs out of the covers and placed her feet on the wooden boards. The sharp cold was almost a relief.

James grunted and shifted position, but he didn't wake up. Dani went over to the dresser under the window, she gently pulled open the drawer and looked at the note again. It's question both benign and sinister at the same time.

She was here because James had asked her. Because she felt she owed him for things that happened in the past. But James owed *her* too. In his mind, he would always be trying to make up for what happened with Tessa Paton. She was an evil and manipulative woman who took James in for a while. Dani had forgiven him, but was well aware he hadn't forgiven himself.

So why had he brought them here? The thought began to niggle that there was something else, an element he was keeping back. As a detective she was trained to pick up on these things; only sentiment, only love, tended to get in the way of these instincts, to muddy and obscure them.

Dani pulled aside the curtain and gazed out into the darkness. The moon was visible in the clear sky and it illuminated the snow on the tree tops. The grounds surrounding the house were still buried beneath a dump of several feet of the white stuff. She groaned, trying to fight that claustrophobic feeling that was constricting her chest once again.

Then she spotted another source of light. A narrow beam was sweeping the trunks of the trees, not far from the house. Dani put her face up to the window, trying to identify its origin. At the source of the beam was a large, dark figure, tracking through the forest at some speed. She gasped. It was a man with a flashlight. Or could it be a woman? She decided not, as the figure was far too tall and broad, even in contrast with the towering pines.

She checked her phone. It was just after 3am. What was he doing out there? Who was he? As she strained to follow the direction he was moving in, the figure abruptly turned, a pale face tilted directly towards her window, as if he had sensed someone watching him.

Dani jerked backward in alarm. Had he seen her there? The figure was stock-still for a moment, then twisted position and set off again into the dark.

Her breathing was rapid. She pulled a woollen blanket off the bed and slumped into the armchair in the corner, swaddling herself in the soft material, her heart still thumping wildly in her chest.

She watched James sleeping soundly, glad he was getting some rest, but knowing for sure there would be no more sleep for her that night.

Chapter 12

Sharon closed the door to the family room softly. She gestured to the DC on the desk closest to the corridor. "Hey, keep an eye on the kid for me, would you? See what kind of carry-out he fancies and order something for yourself."

He nodded with a grin. "Sure thing."

Sharon approached the DCI's office, seeing Dermot seated at the boss's desk through the murky glass partition. She sighed deeply and knocked.

*

The DI's mouth tightened, lines splaying out in tiny crescents at the corners, deepening the further Sharon got through her story. He held up a hand to pause the flow of information. "Hang on, that kid in there isn't one of the gang who burgled the house in Clyde Wharf?"

"Nope, his name is Jackson Fleetwood. He will be fourteen next month. He was in his bedroom when he heard the window being forced downstairs."

"Christ! He must have been terrified!"

"Have you tracked down the rest of the family yet?"

"The neighbour who informed the PC who did the house-to-house that they were holidaying in Tenerife didn't know where they were staying. I've got officers ringing round all the resorts, no luck just yet."

"They're staying at the Europa Sunshine Resort, Santa Cruz. Jackson has his mum's mobile number too."

Dermot rubbed his temple. "Right, I'll get that information over to the team." He looked Sharon in the eye. "Why the hell didn't he tell us all this when

Kev and I manhandled him back to the station? Why was he running away in the first place?"

"Because he thought he'd get into trouble for being in the house on his own, especially over Christmas. Or his parents would."

"Take a seat Sharon, tell me his version of exactly what happened."

She lowered herself into the chair, trying to get her own head around the information she'd received from the tearful teenager. "His parents had booked the Christmas holiday several months back. It's to celebrate his dad's 50th Birthday. There are two younger siblings, aged 8 and 10. Jackson feels like all the activities they do are for the younger ones, it's too childish for him. As the holiday got closer, he told his mum and dad he wouldn't go. There were lots of rows, threats of no Christmas presents, that kind of thing."

"Couldn't he have gone to stay with a relative instead? Grandparents maybe?"

"He's only got a granny and she's in a care home in Largs. I didn't get the impression the family is close to any uncles or aunts."

"Then family friends? Someone surely could have taken him?" Dermot ran his hand through his dark hair, leaving it ruffled.

"It seems Jackson told his parents that a friend of his had invited him to theirs on Christmas Day and he'd sleepover. His dad was refusing to ruin their special holiday because Jackson was being a, quote, "selfish little bastard". So they agreed that he could stay behind, as long as he ate properly and kept out of trouble."

"So who did Jackson stay with on Christmas Day? We're going to need to question them."

"Nobody. The mate who'd offered to have Jackson hadn't told his parents, who understandably, didn't want to share Christmas dinner with another surly teenager. Jackson didn't dare tell them he was on his own in the house so he abandoned the plan. On Christmas Day he ordered KFC from Deliveroo, his parents had left him plenty of cash." Sharon tried to hide the catch in her voice.

"Fucking Hell. Just when you think you've seen it all in this job, something else comes along to surprise you."

"Jackson got the Xbox series x console before they flew out, it was his Christmas present."

"And I bet they thought it would keep him occupied whilst they were away."

Sharon nodded sadly, noting not for the first time that having money didn't guarantee you were a decent person. "He's been playing on it most of the time in his room, chatting to his mates. They've no idea he's on his own. It was lucky Jackson was taking a break when he heard the robbers breaking in. If he'd still had his headphones on they would have entered the house without him even knowing."

Dermot shuddered at the thought. Christ, he wanted to get his hands on those parents.

"He knew it was a break-in, the alarm went off not long after. His parents had shown him how to set it." Sharon continued. "There's a shelf above the built-in wardrobe in his parents' room, he thought his only hope was to hide in there. But he pulled the wires out of his Xbox first and took it with him, along with his iPhone which he stuffed in the pocket of his jeans."

"His prized possessions."

"He clambered up onto the shelf, which runs the length of the wall and pulled down the shelf door which closes like a skylight."

"Yep, I know the type."

"He was pinning his hopes on the burglars being quick, the alarm was already blaring. The worst moment was when he heard them rummaging around the master-suite, he was so scared of them finding him he could hardly breathe."

"How long was the poor sod up there?"

"He doesn't know exactly, but it must have been a few hours. The alarm finally switched itself off and the house seemed quiet, but he was still too terrified to climb down. Then he heard more movement downstairs, so he stayed put."

"That was the officers from the squad car arriving."

"Yep, he worked out it was the police, because he heard the instructions coming from Kev's radio."

"Why didn't he just call out to us, we would have helped him."

"He thought he was in serious trouble *and* his parents. He thought they'd all go to prison because he was at home alone. We may think his mum and dad are tossers, but they're still his family."

"I suppose so, but he finally made a run for it?"

"Jackson isn't silly. He knew we'd be searching everywhere before we left. He heard Kev go out of the bedroom for a minute and decided to make his move. He reckoned he could climb down both balconies and get away. But obviously, Kev heard him and went in pursuit. Although, why he was still gripping that console, I've no idea."

"He was in shock," Dermot explained. "I attended a house once, where there'd been an attempted kidnapping of the family of a top foreign official. The plot was botched in the end, but one of the kids had been hiding in a wardrobe the whole time the kidnappers were in the house. She was gripping a toy doll when we found her, wouldn't let it go for the next 48hrs, not until the counsellor had finally calmed her down."

Sharon glanced across at the door to the family room, feeling her heart swell with sadness for this lad. "Can we prosecute the parents?"

"Yes," Dermot added firmly. "There are no laws stipulating the age at which a child can be left overnight on their own, but the guidance is sixteen. If they are under that age and we deem that they have been placed in danger by being left, which is clearly provable in this case, we can prosecute for neglect."

Sharon didn't reply, she wanted Jackson's mum and dad punished for being so selfish, so weak, but she suspected the boy himself wouldn't feel the same.

Chapter 13

At 7am the radiator beside Dani abruptly creaked into life, waking her from an uncomfortable, light sleep. She sat upright in the chair, a shot of muscular pain exploding in her neck.

"Ow!" She exclaimed, rubbing the muscle and blinking gritty eyes.

James shifted up in the bed. "What are you doing over there? Don't tell me you've been in that chair all night." His tone reflected an element of hurt.

"I couldn't sleep."

"Well, you were never likely to in that armchair."

Dani moved across and sat beside him on the bed. "I saw someone out in the woods last night, a man I think. He was walking around with a flashlight. At 3am."

James rubbed his eyes, feeling the onset of a headache. "It must have been the groundsman. He lives on the edge of the wood, doesn't he?"

"Why would he be out there in the middle of the night?"

James shrugged. "I don't know, tracking wild animals maybe. Did he come near the house?"

"No, he went deeper into the wood."

"It wasn't a would-be intruder then?"

"If someone is casing a property to break into, they can often scout the area several times before they actually commit the burglary."

"Then we'll mention it to Bernie, he must have some CCTV out there. He can report it to the local station."

"No, don't mention it just yet. You're right, there are other people on this estate we haven't even met yet, it could have been anybody."

"Well, okay. But you're the one who usually wants to keep everything by the book. If you see someone acting suspiciously, you report it and give a bloody good description. That could be the testimony which breaks a case."

Dani nodded. She certainly did believe that. In her many years in the job she'd seen it countless times; that one observant person could deliver the evidence that solved a seemingly impossible case. Her body began to relax as the heat from the radiator slowly filled the room. But here, she wasn't a cop. This was the Ravens' private estate, all 12 acres of it. It felt like she didn't have the right or the jurisdiction to interfere. "Let's wait, we're here as visitors, on holiday. I'll ask a few questions first."

"Good." James shifted to the edge of the bed. "Because I'm desperate for a hot shower before breakfast."

Dani smiled, "Me too, and I definitely need some strong coffee to go with it."

*

Breakfast was served in the dining room, where the morning sunlight was spilling in through the bay window onto a refectory table filled with plates of bacon and eggs, cereals and fruit and a cauldron sized bowl of porridge.

Dani filled a large stoneware mug from the coffee machine on the sideboard. She gazed across the snowy lawn to the glittering loch. "If the sun is so bright, why isn't it melting the snow?"

Allan Baxter paused from filling his plate with eggs and toast. "The temperature isn't high enough. The sun may look strong through the glass but it's not powerful enough to shift the ice. Think about skiing resorts in the Alps; the sun can be blinding in winter, but the snow remains intact."

Dani nodded her agreement. "Yes, I see."

Sasha and Oliver entered the room, both in jeans and Fair Isle style knitted jumpers; Sasha with her red hair twisted up in a neat bun.

"Morning, all!" Sasha exclaimed brightly, but her smile didn't quite meet her hazel eyes.

"Good Morning," Helen replied. "I wonder what's in store for us today?"

Sasha dropped onto a chair and reached for the jug of orange juice. "Oh, I know!"

"Well, do tell," Helen replied dryly.

Sasha placed her elbows on the table. "Bernie wanted to take the boat out on the loch and go fishing, but apparently the mooring is frozen solid. So instead we're going to forage on the estate for delicacies that Mrs N will add to our dinner tonight. The groundsman has worked us out a route and will be our guide. Apparently, he's a total Bear Grylls."

"Will we be foraging in the forest?" James asked innocently.

Sasha nodded enthusiastically. "That's where all the mushrooms are and maybe even truffles. It's so protected under the trees, there probably won't even be any snow."

James shot a glance at Dani and raised an eyebrow. She knew he was indicating this could have been the reason for the nocturnal movements of the man dressed in black the previous night. It did make sense, more so than the idea of a random intruder hanging around the estate in sub-zero conditions. She gave him a reassuring smile and sipped her coffee.

"So we all need to wrap up warm," Sasha concluded.

Tony didn't look impressed, he and Dotty were seated at the other end of the table, quietly eating their porridge. "I think it will be too cold for my wife," he said weakly.

"Oh, I'm sure nobody is expecting Dorothy to come with us," Helen chimed. "She's already got a chill."

Tony's lined face sagged with relief. "You can stay here, darling," he whispered to her, like she was a child.

"Why isn't Bernie here telling us all this himself?" Allan demanded good-naturedly. "Not like him to have a lie-in!"

"I expect he's helping to set the trail," Sasha added defensively. "I'm only repeating what Morag told me earlier. Our room is close to theirs. She wanted me to pass it on."

"And we're glad you did," Dani said levelly. "What time do we need to meet?" Somehow Dani felt the younger woman would know this information, that Morag was using her as a go-between with the rest of the group.

"We meet at 10.30am in the main hall," Sasha delivered the words with a little less gusto, as if realising this fact for the first time herself.

Chapter 14

Detective Chief Superintendent Ronnie Douglas was standing in DCI Bevan's cramped office, his tall, broad figure making the room even smaller. He wasn't in uniform, just a pair of beige corduroy trousers and a Ben Sherman shirt.

"Jackson Fleetwood is 13 years and 11 months old. The child psychologist passed onto me the psychological assessment she performed this morning."

Sharon and Dermot listened in silence, they were happy for the DCS to take the lead on this.

"He's under extreme stress, due to being at a police station and fearing his parents are about to be arrested. There is evidence of psychological trauma relating to the shock of the break-in at his house, but the psych reckons with some decent counselling, his long term prognosis is good. He's intelligent and articulate, has long periods of being calm and reflective and otherwise has no immediate physical or mental health needs."

"Good," Sharon said with feeling. "So, what happens next?"

Douglas glanced at his watch. "It's mid-morning on the 27th December. The chances of securing him a temporary foster home before the New Year are nil. Child Protection are seeing if they have a bed spare at Heath Mount."

"The children's home?" Sharon said the words with disdain.

"Yes, the *residential youth care facility*. There will be staff on duty 24hrs a day and they have a resident counsellor. He'll be safe there."

Sharon knitted her brow, uncomfortable with the idea.

Dermot interrupted. "The family have been located at the Hotel Europol in Tenerife. A local officer has made contact, but the mother isn't answering her mobile phone when we try and call."

Douglas grunted. "She knows we're onto them. How soon can we get them back in the UK?"

"Our liaison, who speaks very good English due to Tenerife being full of Brits, says Steve Fleetwood is being difficult. He's refusing to change his flight. We don't have the jurisdiction to arrest them over there until we've been granted a European Arrest Warrant, but the local Policia are being very helpful. I had hoped they'd return voluntarily as the charge isn't that serious and they have family and jobs back home to return to. Steve is a chief mechanic for one of the BMW showrooms on the outskirts of the city. Liz works part-time on the reception of her youngest children's primary school."

"The EAW has been applied for and is under consideration. When were the family due to come back from the holiday anyway?" Douglas's tone was flint-like.

"New Year's Day, Sir."

"And they know their house has been burgled whilst their son was inside? That he hid on his own from the intruders for several hours?"

"Yes, Sir. They also know that as soon as they land on Scottish soil, we will be there to arrest them and possibly take their younger two children into immediate care, which complicates matters I suppose."

Sharon felt the blood pumping behind her eyes, a sense of mounting rage building the pressure. "Why didn't they jump on the next available plane when they found out what happened to Jackson?"

Dermot sighed. "Well, he's actually safer now than he was before the break-in. I can sort of see their twisted logic."

Douglas rubbed his bald pate. "I bet they're playing for time so they can sort out a lawyer to meet them when they land at Prestwick, get themselves some advice before we start the interviews. The EAW always takes time to raise and at this time of year…" He blew out his cheeks, then the DCS seemed to suddenly have an idea. "Dermot, get your team to check they haven't got any family or friends living in Spain who can shelter them, especially on one of the Canary Islands. If they decide to go on the run with the younger kids, we've got an almighty mess on our hands."

Dermot's expression darkened as he nodded in confirmation that this would, indeed, be a disaster.

*

Sharon had brought Jackson out onto the serious crime floor of the Pitt Street station. She felt he couldn't be shut up in the family room on his own any longer, considering how alone he'd been over the previous few days.

A few of the DCs were scattered about the sea of desks, but they were still very much on a skeleton staff. A few snakes of tinsel had been draped around the light fittings and a framed portrait of the Queen that the DCS insisted they display. The place had a shabbily festive feel to it.

Jackson took the seat opposite Sharon at her work station. His expression was miserable and his posture stooped. "The Detective Chief Superintendent is looking into a place for you to stay tonight. It will be safe and comfortable, I promise."

The boy shrugged. "When are my family getting back? I've tried ringing Mum a dozen times and she's not picking up." His tone was apparently uninterested, but he plucked nervously at the seam of his jeans as he asked the question.

"It's complicated. New flights need to be arranged. Your mum has probably been told not to take any calls by the local police." Sharon knew this wasn't likely to be true, but she couldn't break this boy's heart any more times.

"I'd thought they'd be back by tonight, the flight's only 4hrs or so? I looked up alternatives on my phone."

Dani inwardly cringed. She didn't think this lad could take any more rejection. "It's not their fault, they've got to be questioned by the police over there before they can be released to come home. You know what these places are like, nightmare bureaucracy."

Jackson narrowed his eyes, as if aware Sharon was obfuscating, but he didn't press the issue.

"Now, what's your best subject at school?" She asked brightly, hoping to divert his attention.

"DT, I'm good at making things. We've got a cool 3D printer in the department."

"How about Geography?"

He shifted up a fraction higher in his seat. "It's one of my Highers subjects. My teacher thinks I'm okay at it."

"Well then, maybe you can assist me with some policework?"

Jackson looked suspicious again. "I don't think you're meant to let me do that. It's all confidential and stuff. I still don't reckon you're a proper cop." His words were harsh but they were spoken with a twinkle of humour in those green-grey eyes.

"This is strictly 'off the books'." Sharon reached for an ordnance survey map in one of the drawers. "Do you know what this is?"

"*Of course*, we use them on DofE hikes."

"Good. This one covers Beinn Dearg and Loch Broom, in the Western Highlands. Do you know it?"

"We had a holiday once near Gairloch."

"Good. Now, my boss is on holiday up there right now, in a house on the banks of Loch Broom, I've marked it on the map."

The boy raised his eyebrows. "At *this* time of year?"

"Well, as you will know, the weather hasn't been great here in Glasgow, but the snowfall has been even more severe up there." She opened the map and placed it on his side of the desk. "I want you to take a look at routes in and out, all the transport links and whether they're running, and check the weather, hour by hour on the Met office app using your phone. Can you manage that?"

"Yeah, sure I can. Just like DofE. But why do you want me to do it, is your boss in some kind of trouble?"

Sharon sat back down in her seat with a bump. "Not yet, but I've just got a funny feeling she might find herself needing a quick route out of there. I want to be able to provide it for her."

Chapter 15

The group had assembled at the foot of the grand staircase. Dani glanced at her reflection in the large antique mirror hanging in the hall. Her face was pale and under her eyes, dark smudges were the legacy of her sleepless night.

James had come down before her and she looked around to see where he was. All the other guests, apart from Dotty, were there. The Prestons were in brightly coloured ski-wear and the Baxters had on thick woollen coats and Hunter wellies. Dani and James had packed walking boots and puffy North Face jackets which they had paired with hats and thermal gloves.

The only person who seemed ill-attired for their trek was Tony. He wore a thin anorak, cords and a pair of battered brogues.

Before Dani could comment on Tony's choice of outdoor clothing, Bernie breezed into the room, decked out from head to foot in the very top brands of outdoor gear. A few seconds later, James followed on, a pinched expression on his face.

Dani shot him a questioning look, but he turned his head, avoiding her gaze.

Bernie boomed, "glad to see you all ready for our woodland trek! Morag and I have been considering running some local events from out of the castle. One of them is a gourmet weekend, including foraging for some of the ingredients and a few well-chosen woodland activities. So, if you don't mind, you lot will be our first guinea-pigs." He laughed to take any sting out of his words.

"I just hope you know what you're doing, Bernie," Allan put in. "Some of the plants in the forests are highly poisonous to humans and animals. I've lost count of the number of dogs' stomachs I've had to pump over the years after eating a toxic mushroom or two and those were the lucky ones."

Bernie brushed away the vet's concern with a wave of his broad arm. "Peter Tredegar, my groundsman, is leading the expedition. He is highly trained in Highland survival techniques. He won't let us pick anything that's going to kill us, don't you worry!"

Somehow, Dani didn't feel entirely reassured. Looking at the faces of her fellow guests, she wasn't sure they were either. Only Sasha seemed oblivious, as if she wasn't really listening to her uncle at all.

Bernie finally noticed Tony Shannahan, who was almost crouching behind the rest of the group. "Tony, you'll catch your death out there dressed like that." His tone was solicitous, almost gentle. "We've got plenty of spare gear in the boot room. I'll get Morag to dig you something out." He turned to the rest of them, his overbearing personality once again in evidence. "Whilst we do that, take yourselves into Mrs N's kitchen, she's got some baskets for you to collect all your goodies in."

*

In her deep red puffer jacket and with a wicker basket slotted over her arm, setting off into the woods, Dani felt like Little Red Riding Hood. She would have joked about it with James, but he was walking stiffly beside her, still avoiding her eye.

They trudged along a path that had been cleared of snow towards a set of outhouses which were nestled into the edge of the forest. Dani breathed in deeply. The air was crisp and fresh, smelling of pine needles and wood smoke, it was a typical Highland aroma that she loved. The loch lay absolutely still in the distance.

The groundsman emerged from a stone lodge which sat apart from the barns, at the beginning of a path into the woods. He looked to be in his forties, wearing a dark jacket and waterproof trousers with a sturdy pair of black boots. His face was rugged but handsome. Dani wondered if this could have been the man she saw in the woods the previous night. It was certainly possible.

He strode out to greet them. "I'm Pete Tredegar, the groundsman at Strathain House. Bernie has provided me with all your details, but forgive me if I get some names muddled up." He nodded his head towards his boss.

Dani scanned the group. Tony was now wearing a garish purple and white ski jacket and welly boots. He didn't look happy to be there. In fact, the only ones who were showing any outward enthusiasm were Sasha and Oliver, who were clasping one another's hands and sharing jokes. She felt a pang, that would have been her and James once. She wondered what the hell was wrong with him. Since breakfast he'd barely said a word.

"It's too cold to hang around," Pete said firmly. "Follow my lead and I'll tell you exactly what we're looking for as we go." He turned and headed purposefully along the winding woodland path, the rest of the group trailing along behind him.

Chapter 16

Jackson released the ring-pull on a can of coke he'd found in the department fridge. He sipped the fizzy liquid as he examined the map laid out on Sharon's desk. The DS had gone off to speak with her boss in his office.

The area he'd been tasked with surveying was full of forests, mountains and lochs. Just the sort of terrain it was difficult to navigate with any speed. He remembered the family holiday they'd had in Gairloch. It was when his brother and sister were still only wee. They'd rented a cottage facing Longa Island. His dad had taken him fishing in a boat on the loch, just the two of them. Jackson's eyes misted with tears. He brushed them away fiercely. What an idiot he'd been. Why hadn't he just agreed to go on holiday with them this time? Why had he been so moody, so uncooperative, to the point where his parents were prepared to leave him at home, maybe even relieved to do so?

A tear pooled in his eye and dripped onto the map. He took a gulp of coke to try and shift the lump that had formed in his throat. He wouldn't let Sharon see him like this, although she seemed a nice lady and probably wouldn't mind. The other cops and that psychologist would see it as a sign of serious mental trauma and cart him off to some residential home. It wasn't trauma he was suffering from, just the realisation he'd been a bloody fool, immature and jealous of his two younger siblings.

He took a deep breath and turned his attention back to the map. Only one road ran past the east bank of Loch Broom, the A835. This was the road which passed Strathain House, where the police woman was staying.

According to the local traffic reports, which he'd been following on his phone, this road was blocked by heavy snow in both directions. The weather report indicated there would be another heavy dumping overnight when temperatures could get as low as -4 degrees. He shivered at the thought. Snowfall would begin again at around sundown, which was due at 15:48pm.

He jotted this information down on a pad of paper Sharon gave him. The nearest town to this Highland castle was Inverlael, which was itself temporarily cut off from the larger towns to the north, like Ullapool and Oykel Bridge. But at least Inverlael had shops and a small supermarket, which would presumably keep them going for a while.

Sharon had told him that her boss had no Internet coverage or mobile phone reception at Strathain House. They could only use the landline. But Jackson checked the area for its broadband coverage. In fact, high speed lines had been fitted to the house the previous year, by a contractor for the Scottish government. They'd also dug up pavements all through Inverlael at the same time. He saw there'd been umpteen complaints sent to the council offices in Inverness about the disruption.

But that didn't really matter, the point was that even with the bad weather, the place should still have had broadband. It was true the mobile phone network had a weak signal up there and the weather had probably knocked out the mast. But Sharon's boss should have been able to get Internet still.

Jackson yawned. He'd barely slept since his parents left. He stayed up most of Christmas night playing on his X-box, he didn't have anyone nagging him to turn it off, or telling him he should go to bed.

It had been blissful, until he heard those burglars breaking in downstairs on Boxing Day morning. Then he wasn't quite so gleeful at being on his own. His chest tightened and he felt the tips of his fingers tingle at the memory.

He distracted himself from the unpleasant thoughts by looking up the transport systems for the area. The Highland bus network were grounded by the weather, although they'd normally pass by the front of Strathain House. The nearest train station was at Achanalt, which was 25 miles away and pretty much unreachable by road.

Of course, there was the ferry from Ullapool to Stornoway, and from there to the other Hebridean islands, but you'd have to reach the ferry port first and as far as Jackson could tell, all the Cal Mac ferries were moored up until the weather improved. He sighed deeply, he really wanted to find a solution for Sharon, make himself useful so they didn't cart him off to some hostel.

He felt the tears welling up again, so he turned determinedly back to the map, losing himself in those mountains and forests, looking closely at paths and trails, imaging himself in that cold, Highland landscape, in the hope of coming across a way out.

Chapter 17

The forest was dense with towering fir trees, but Dani was grateful for the absence of snow. They could walk without effort on the spongy soil of the forest floor which was covered with a blanket of decaying pine needles. The evergreen foliage was also insulating them from the bitter cold. It was much milder beneath the canopy of the trees than out in the open and as they walked, she found herself warming up.

Pete led them to a small clearing amongst the trees. "At this time of year, we would expect to be able to collect a good selection of winter fruits and nuts. We're talking acorns, blackberries and chestnuts. At the edge of the forest, in the hedgerows, we may be lucky enough to find some bullace fruit that is ripened. It's a type of plum that is native to this area and can still be found as late as January."

"What about mushrooms?" Asked Oliver. "I thought that was what foraging was all about finding?"

Pete smiled. "Not at this time of year. If the Ravens do have paying guests to come on these expeditions, the best time is going to be October for the mushrooms."

Oliver looked disappointed.

Pete gave a good-natured laugh. "The outdoors is not like a supermarket, where we get produce all year round, transported from all over the world. Here we get what is seasonal and make the best use of it. That's the beauty of Nature, really."

"So, what *should* we be looking for now?" James sounded uncharacteristically impatient.

Pete raised his arm up to one of the branches beside him, he pulled off a handful of the emerald pine needles. "These beauties for a start, James. The needles can be infused to make tea. They're full of vitamin C and Vitamin A, to help you see in the dark."

Dani was sure she saw the groundsman glance at her as he made this statement, a glint of humour in his eyes. Had he spotted her watching him in the forest the previous night? Was he mocking her for attempting to hide from him, for her fear of his nocturnal activities?

"So, go ahead, get some needles into your baskets. They must be fresh, straight off the tree. And whilst you're here, look out for pine cones, they have seeds in the centre that we can roast and sprinkle on a salad."

The group moved around the clearing in silence, filling their baskets with needles and cones. Dani positioned herself beside James. "Is everything okay? You disappeared off this morning after breakfast."

He seemed suddenly intent on the job of sliding a handful of pine needles off a branch. "I wanted to catch Bernie before we set off on this trek. I knew I wouldn't get any time with him once we were together as a group."

"What did you want to talk about?"

James shot her a glance, a flash of irritation in his expression. "Work, of course. I know you're having an awful time. You slept in a bloody chair last night. I was the one who dragged you here. I thought the least I could do was try and get some more business out of Bernie. That is supposed to be the point of this whole trip."

Dani laid a hand on his shoulder. "I'm sorry, that note under our door just unsettled me. You really don't have to worry about fighting for contracts whilst we're here." She gazed about the forest, where beams of sun were filtering through the canopy above, bathing them in golden light and breathed in the heady scent of pine. "Look at the scenery around us. Let's just enjoy it, eh?"

James's lips cracked into a smile. "I'd really like to. This is actually my kind of thing."

She leant against his body, heavily padded by his jacket. "I know it is."

"Got enough produce from the pines?" Pete called out. "Then let's keep moving folks."

The groundsman led them along the winding path, until the pine forest thinned out and the trees surrounding them became more varied in appearance.

He led them to the trunk of a shorter, wider tree with almost bare, interconnected branches. "Anyone know what tree this is?"

"A Chestnut," Allan replied swiftly. "There are lots in the valley of Loch Broom."

Pete smiled broadly. "Correct. Now this collection of Chestnuts are extra special, because they are completely sheltered to the north by the pine forest, towering above them. So they bear fruit much later than would usually be expected. Look down at your feet."

They dutifully obeyed. Dani noticed the collection of spiky green parcels she remembered from her early youth in the forests of Wales.

Pete scooped a couple up in his hands. "It's late in the season, so they should just come apart in your hands. Don't let the prickles put you off. Inside is a smooth nut which has multiple culinary uses." He nodded to Tony, who was gazing out into the wood, not appearing to be taking any notice of the talk. "Why don't you pick one up and try?"

The older man turned his head back to Pete abruptly, reaching down and picking up a spiky ball. He gazed at it with bemusement, like it was alive and might bite his hand.

"Try peeling back the outer shell," Pete suggested. "Or if the spikes really put you off, find a stone and give it a gentle knock."

Tony dropped his to the floor, as if it was burning his hand and abruptly stamped on it with his welly boot. When he removed his foot, the ball had split open but the nut inside had also been crushed into a mess of brown and white pulp.

"Okay Tony, that's one way of doing it!" Pete kept his tone light, but there was a hint of annoyance there anyway. "But remember, we want to keep those precious little nuts inside. Mrs Noble will be cooking you roast loin of venison this evening, with a chestnut purée and seasonal vegetables. For dessert, there will be chocolate and chestnut truffle torte. *You*, will be providing the chestnuts."

Sasha squealed in delight and clapped her hands. "Come on, let's make it a competition?! Who can collect the most?!"

Pete laughed. "Great idea, Sasha. We've got about twenty minutes here until we move onto our next activity, which I think you're going to really love."

Chapter 18

When Sharon returned to her desk she was impressed by the volume of notes Jackson had made. As a distraction activity, it had seemed to work pretty well.

She listened patiently as the teenager relayed the information he had so far garnered, her brow knitting with concern as he mentioned the fully functioning broadband cable recently connected to the Strathain estate.

"Are you sure about that?" She asked.

He looked affronted. "Yeah, course I am. The broadband rollout is all catalogued online. Anyone can go on the website and have a look. The government are quite proud of how it's going, especially to rural areas."

Sharon nodded. "I'm sure it is. I'm just wondering why the owners of Strathain House told their guests they didn't have any Wi-Fi?"

Jackson shrugged. "Maybe they wanted them to get away from distractions whilst they were on holiday. Sometimes, my mum pulls out the plug on our Wi-Fi if she can't get me off the Xbox. She says it's for my own good." He cleared his throat, hoping he didn't start crying again.

"Yes, but these guests are adults – no offence – some of them will have children, elderly parents who they may need to contact in an emergency." She ran a hand through her messy curls, which she'd made no real effort to control as it was Christmas week.

"Well, the mobile reception *is* really bad. I remember that from our holiday in Gairloch. Dad moaned about it the whole week."

At least that element was true. Sharon was about to press Jackson more on his findings, when she spotted DCS Douglas emerging from the lift. She excused herself and moved across the floor to intercept him.

Douglas lowered his tone. "How's the boy doing?"

"I've given him some tasks to keep him occupied, but he'll need feeding again soon."

"You make him sound like an infant." Douglas couldn't help but smile.

"Well, teenagers need constant feeding, don't they? My sister's two certainly do. It's just he's been eating takeaways since his parents left. It's about time he had some decent home cooked food. He's pale enough as it is."

Douglas nodded solemnly. "I've not got great news on that front."

Sharon's heart sank, she glanced across at the boy's stooped figure, intent on the map laid in front of him.

"The foster parent route will take weeks. I'm afraid there are currently no beds at the residential home."

Dermot had walked up to join them, listening to the DCS's words. "So what are the other options?"

"Well, his parents are still in the Canaries and a temporary removal order is being drawn up for Jackson and his siblings whilst the case is considered by Child Services. Unfortunately, Jackson will have to be placed in a B&B until other accommodation can be found."

Sharon gasped. "He'll be completely unsupervised, with nowhere to cook a meal and no one to look after him."

"It's not ideal, I realise. But the time of year is most unfortunate."

Sharon felt her blood pressure rising again. "Can he come and stay with me, at my flat? It's only going to be temporary, right?"

Douglas sighed. He had sensed this might be coming. DS Moffett had always struck him as a little unorthodox, but Bevan seemed to highly rate her. "It's highly unusual for a police officer to take on temporary foster care, but it isn't unheard of."

Sharon's face brightened. "Then it's a possibility?"

"Think about this carefully, Sharon," Dermot interrupted. "This kid has been through a tricky time. His own parents obviously found him difficult to handle. Taking him home is way beyond the job remit."

She turned to her colleague. "It's snowing outside and freezing cold. There's no way that boy can go to a crumbling hotel on his own. You tell me an alternative."

Dermot shrugged. "I haven't got one." He sighed. "If you take him home to your place, I'll help. We can look after him in shifts and bring him into the department with us."

"What will Serena say?" Sharon asked in surprise.

"Plenty," Dermot replied dryly.

Douglas raised a hand. "Hold on, there are procedures here. An officer from Child Services will have to come over to Pitt Street and assess both of you. Of course, you are fully vetted as serving police officers, but she will want to weigh up your motives and suitability to look after a vulnerable boy."

"Okay, fine. Just let me know when I can see her."

Douglas sighed at Sharon's impulsiveness, but he was also deeply relieved. He couldn't have allowed the lad to spend even a night in one of the badly maintained, ill-equipped hotels the council used to house the temporarily dispossessed. They were noisy and frightening at night according to the many complaints he'd read from asylum seekers and families fleeing domestic abuse, desperate for temporary shelter. If Sharon hadn't offered, he'd have done it himself and Mrs Douglas would not have been best pleased. He made eye contact with both officers, quietly proud of them. "Right, I'll get it organised."

Chapter 19

As the group made their way deeper into the forest, Dani heard the sound of footsteps behind them, drumming against the soft ground, vibrating through the earth under their feet.

Bernie had caught up with them with a relative ease considering his age. "I'm glad I found you before the big event," he called.

Dani hadn't even noticed he'd dropped back.

Pete stopped and turned, clearly not surprised to see his boss making a re-appearance. "We've got plenty of produce to bring back for Mrs N. All straight from 'Nature's kitchen'."

Dani was beginning to tire of the groundsman's naturalistic spiel, but she supposed it would appeal to tourists. She wondered why Bernie had joined them now and not earlier, perhaps foraging for nuts and seeds wasn't really up his street? He was the CEO of one of the highest ranking companies in the UK. He probably wasn't used to making his own meals, let alone scraping around undergrowth for the ingredients.

Bernie patted James on the back as he made his way to the head of the party. Dani was sure she felt her boyfriend shrink from his touch.

They hadn't walked much further when they reached the edge of the forest. A hill stretched off ahead of them, covered in snow. At the foot of the incline was what looked like a newly built construction. A wooden building was surrounded by a spiked fence of freshly cut and sanded pine.

Pete got a bunch of keys out of the pocket of his walking trousers and opened a gate in the fence. As they followed him inside, it became clearer what this area had been designed for.

A hut ran along the rear, with a log roof which provided a canopy for shade and to keep the rain off. Seating had been built around the edge. The hut faced a large fenced-off area about 60 or 70 feet long. The ground had been covered in wood chippings and at the far end stood a series of large and imposing circular targets.

Pete gathered them round him and closed the gate. "Completed only last month, this is the new archery range on the Strathain estate."

Bernie puffed up his chest proudly. "It is constructed from materials found only in this forest and glen."

"We hope to be able to provide the kind of experience that would have been common when Strathain was first built as a highland hunting lodge. But with a more modern, sustainable twist. We will be providing target and field archery for future guests, along with what we are going to be trying our hand at today; axe-throwing."

A thrum of nervous chatter passed through the group.

"Don't worry, we use specially designed axes and unique targets. It's been all the rage in the States and is starting to catch on over here in a big way. It's lots of fun and very therapeutic." Bernie winked at nobody in particular.

"I've done it before," James added cautiously, "whilst on a business trip to Chicago a couple of years ago."

"Great," Pete declared. "Then we aren't all complete beginners."

Before they could think much more about it, Pete organised them into pairs and opened up an equipment shed. As the odd ones out, Bernie and

Tony were placed together, making an incongruous couple.

They were given eye protectors and flak jackets which reminded Dani of the anti-stab vests they used very occasionally at Pitt Street.

Pete carefully hooked up one of the axes from a wooden crate which he held up to show them. "They are shorter handled than the sort of axe you would use to chop wood. I sharpened them all this morning, so do not touch the blade." He made eye contact with them all as he said this.

"Each of you will take a turn, one-by-one. When the throwing is taking place, the rest of us will stay behind this red line." He indicated a red strip of rubber which had been hammered into the ground about six feet out from where they stood.

Pete proceeded to give them clear instructions on how the axe should be handled and thrown. Demonstrating himself by tossing the axe towards one of the large targets. It spun in the air before striking the wood on one of the outer rings. "Not a great score," he added with a grin. "But we are all pretty new to this sport. Give me a bow and arrow, on the other hand, and it will be a bullseye every time."

The groundsman decided to let James and Dani go first, as James already had some experience. Dani could see her partner was putting all his concentration into the task. He lowered his goggles and tossed with all his might. The axe hit the target on one of the outer rings.

"Well done!" Bernie boomed from further down the line. "Our very first score on the board!"

Dani had some target practice firearms training a few years back, so she was used to maintaining a good line. The axe was much quieter and didn't have the kick-back of a pistol, so she felt more comfortable in this scenario. But the technique was tricky and she managed only to strike the outer area of the target, although the axe did bury itself satisfyingly deeply into the soft wood.

"Excellent first attempt, Dani. Now, as we discussed, nobody goes to retrieve their axe until the final pair have thrown, okay?" Pete nodded to the Baxters, indicating it was their turn.

Both had a reasonable attempt. Helen's throw hit the target, whilst Allan's fell a couple of feet short, landing with a thud on the wood chips. He looked a little embarrassed.

Bernie stepped forward eagerly next, obviously having practised on a previous occasion. His throw hit just one row out from the bullseye. Their host pumped his fist in celebration.

By contrast, Tony held the axe limply and Pete had to intervene as he swung the object in a way which suggested he might be aiming for his fellow teammate rather than the target. In the end, Pete held the axe along with the older man and they threw it together. It knocked against the target but couldn't get a purchase on the smooth surface, slipping unceremoniously to the ground.

"Okay, final pair!" Pete announced.

Sasha picked up the axe and pulled down her goggles, a look of fierce concentration on her face. She swung the axe just as Pete had advised them and her throw landed decisively to the right of the bullseye.

"Well done! Pete called out, "if that's your first try, you're a bloody natural!"

Oliver stepped forward, Dani sensed he was as competitive in these situations as his wife. He bit his upper lip as he lined up his position and took aim. He swung with some force, his impressive upper arm muscles having been revealed after removing his padded jacket. The axe spun through the air in a tall ark, it was clearly heading directly for the centre of the target. Helen Baxter clapped with enthusiasm.

But as the axe blade shot towards the bullseye, Dani noticed the glint of something on the target that she'd not noticed on the others. It was like the flash of sunlight on metal. Something, a sort of instinct of danger, made her stretch up on her toes and sprint towards the Prestons.

As the axe blade hit, there was an unnatural metallic clunk, which rang out around the glen. Instead of the dull thud of the axe embedding itself into the pine, the blade ricocheted off the target and began flying back towards the area where the group were standing. Sasha let out a piercing scream.

Dani made a quick calculation. She barged Allan Baxter out of the way and launched herself at Oliver Preston, barrelling him to the ground. Just as their bodies hit the earth, the spinning axe whizzed over their heads, hitting the back wall of the hut with an ear-splitting crack.

Chapter 20

Dani rolled to the side, her heart pounding in her chest and her breath coming in shallow gasps. James fell to his knees beside her and held her in his arms.

"Are you okay?"

Dani sat up and looked for Oliver. "I'm fine, just pumped full of adrenaline and a little bruised. Is anyone hurt?" She called out.

Oliver had levered himself up on his elbows, winded and shocked but otherwise unscathed. "What the hell happened?"

Pete was rapidly by their side. "There was something metal on the target, the axe blade bounced straight off it and came shooting back towards the safe area."

"Wasn't so *safe* after all," Allan said dryly, his expression grim.

"I don't know how on earth this happened," Pete entreated. "I checked all the equipment, including the targets first thing this morning. Hell, I was up all night getting this bloody trek together. I was even in the woods in the early hours scattering chestnuts around the clearing so we had enough for the dinner tonight. I left absolutely nothing to chance!".

Dani looked around for Bernie, who should really have been the one dealing with this debacle. She saw that he had made his way over to the far target, where Oliver's axe had struck. He was running his large hand over the surface of the bullseye. "It's some kind of metal staple," He called out. "The damn thing has been driven right into the wood."

Pete and James jogged over. They watched as Bernie pulled a pen-knife out of his pocket and began levering the staple from the wood, seemingly not caring that his actions were causing the surface to splinter and break.

Dani got shakily to her feet. "Hey! You shouldn't be touching that! This could be a crime scene. That staple must have been put in the target deliberately."

Bernie swivelled on his heels. "How can that be the case?" His eyes were bright with anger. "It was just a freak accident. I've got to get this thing out before someone else gets hurt." He waved the blade around before jamming it back into the wood behind the staple and gouging violently.

Pete placed his hand on his boss's shoulder. "Bernie," he said in a gentle tone. "Dani's right. That staple was placed there by someone. It wasn't there when I checked the equipment at 9am. I can swear to that. The range was locked up until we arrived here at noon. But let's be honest, someone could have climbed over the fence to gain access, if they wanted to enough."

Bernie shook his head in bewilderment, but he stopped hacking at the offending piece of metal. "But *who* would want to do that? And *why*?"

Dani walked back towards the others. Helen and Allan were fussing over Oliver, who was still seated on the ground, examining his grazed palms. She gazed past them at Sasha instead, who was standing in the shadow of the hut, her hands covering her face, rocking in distress.

"Sasha? Are you okay? Oliver is alright you know, we got out of the way in time." Dani moved closer, staring at the younger woman who seemed in some anguish.

Sasha stepped unsteadily out of the shadows, dropping her hands down to her sides.

Dani let out a gasp. A long, diagonal gash was visible along her forehead, just above her left eye and her face was streaked with bright crimson blood.

*

When they arrived back at the house, Pete burst through the kitchen door and manoeuvred Sasha into one of the carver chairs at the head of the worn oak table. Allan had gone to fetch his medical bag from their car and followed them in a few seconds later.

He pulled some sheets of paper from a kitchen roll that Mrs Noble handed him and proceeded to gently dab the wound.

"She's not a horse, you realise," Bernie said unpleasantly. "She's my niece."

Allan ignored the comment and continued his work.

Helen rummaged in her husband's bag. "Yes, we're fully aware of that, thank you Bernie. But a nasty cut is the same on an animal or a human. We need to get the area cleaned, get some antiseptic on it and assess whether stitches are required. It looks to me to be a superficial graze. The initial blood loss always makes it seem worse."

Bernie grunted. "My apologies, Helen. I've just had a shock and I'm worried about Sasha. I've not looked after her properly. Her mother won't be pleased."

Morag announced her arrival with the characteristic click-clack of heels echoing somewhere on the ground floor of the house. When she arrived in the doorway, all eyes were turned in her direction.

"What on earth has happened?" She looked straight at Sasha. "Good God. Somebody fetch this girl a brandy."

"That's not a bad idea," Allan said. "She's still shaking badly."

James exited the kitchen. Heading for the drinks cabinet in the dining room they'd used the previous evening.

Tony also rushed from the room. Dani expected it was to go and see his wife, tell her what a lucky escape she'd had by missing the morning's activities.

Dani sank into one of the chairs herself, a wave of exhaustion flowing through her stiff limbs.

Oliver was standing beside his wife, clasping her hand. "In the excitement, I haven't had the chance to thank you, Dani. You saved my life."

"I was convinced you were in the path of the axe, maybe it was Sasha I should have rugby tackled to the floor?"

"No," Helen added forcefully. "That axe was heading straight for Oliver. It would have killed him instantly had you not pushed him out of the way. We were all looking at the two of you and nobody was paying attention to poor Sasha. I think she must have moved to protect Oliver herself, that's why the axe nicked her head as it passed."

"I am still here, you know," Sasha said with a weak voice. "Actually, I'm not sure what happened. When I saw that axe spinning towards us I was terrified. I must have tried to shift out of the way and found myself in its path." She shuddered, wrapping her arms around her thin shoulders.

James arrived with a tumbler of brandy, he placed it directly into Sasha's hand. "Just try a small sip, it will make you feel better and warm you up a little."

She smiled gratefully.

Morag shook her head gravely. "I was never happy about the idea of 'axe-throwing'. I told you it was dangerous."

Bernie scowled. "I'm going to get myself a brandy. Anyone want to join me?" His question was met with silence. "Oh well, suit yourselves." He swept from the room.

Pete addressed Morag. "It should have been perfectly safe. I'd checked and double-checked. We think it was some kind of sabotage."

She huffed, seemingly unconvinced. "How can that be what happened? We are five miles from Inverlael and the road is blocked. I've been sitting by the bay window in the drawing room all morning and not a single soul has approached the house. The snow is as smooth and untouched as a freshly iced Christmas cake. It's too cold for anyone to be hiking in those hills around us. There are the twelve of us here in this house. Nobody else." She threw her hands up in the air. "If anyone sabotaged your forest games it would have to be one of us, wouldn't it? And why on earth would we, eh? Answer me that."

If this statement was designed to put the rest of the group at ease, Dani feared their hostess had failed. Morag's words allowed a seed of doubt and suspicion to germinate somewhere in Dani's brain and she wasn't sure the unpleasant idea, now planted, was likely to go away.

Chapter 21

Dermot slid his body carefully out from behind the TV unit and rubbed his lower back. "I think I've got it plugged in correctly, you'll have to start it up and see."

Jackson couldn't hide the smile that was spreading across his face. He grabbed the controller with unsuppressed glee. "What's your Wi-Fi password, Sharon?"

The DS emerged from her kitchenette with two steaming mugs of coffee. She set them down on a side table. "It's on the front of the Hub, on the hall table."

Whilst he was out of the room, Sharon whispered, "is this such a good idea?"

Dermot shrugged. "Forensics had returned the X-box to us, it's his private property."

"I know, but I don't want him to spend hours and hours on it and bury his problems." Sharon sipped her coffee.

"He's had a very rough few days, a bit of familiarity and escapism won't do him any harm. Plus, the console is connected to your TV, you will get to tell him when to come off, and make sure he gets to bed at a decent time."

"How do I do that?" For the first time, Sharon felt daunted by the task she'd taken on.

Dermot laughed. "I haven't got a clue. I think that's why parenting is so difficult."

Jackson re-entered. "What's so funny?"

"Nothing worth sharing," Sharon said lightly. "There's a coffee here for you, one sugar. Are you connected?"

"Great, thanks. Yep, looks like it. I've got loads of un-read messages from my mates. I'd better get on and answer them."

"Don't tell them about your current situation, will you? The investigation is still ongoing."

"I won't," he muttered, before pulling on his earphones and tuning out the rest of the room.

Dermot shuffled forward on the sofa. "I'd better get back to the department. Are you okay on your own for a few hours?"

"Sure, I can catch up on some paperwork. I'll take Jackson out for a walk later, encourage him to stretch his legs. I'll need to visit the mini-mart anyway, get some fresh food in."

"Sounds like a plan." Dermot rose to his feet. "I'll drop by later and make sure everything is okay."

"Great, much appreciated."

"I'll let myself out." Dermot walked to the door of Sharon's flat and exited into the cramped hallway. It felt strange to be coming and going from his colleague's home in this way, they barely knew one another outside of work.

Dermot and Serena's flat was about a mile away from this building. It wouldn't be too difficult to divide his time between the two, besides, his fiancé was still staying with her parents until New Year. She knew he was on duty and didn't think it was worth coming back to an empty flat. He was glad. It meant he hadn't had to tell her about him and Sharon taking responsibility for Jackson. He hoped it would be temporary, then she'd never have to know about it at all. Something told him she wouldn't be happy about the news, not one little bit.

*

Mrs Noble had prepared a simple lunch of vegetable soup and homemade soda bread. Dani did her best to eat it, knowing her body needed the sustenance after the morning's exertions and shocking events, but her stomach was tied in knots.

She glanced around the dining table, noting that their fellow guests were also finding it hard to tuck in with any great gusto.

Allan put down his spoon. "I do recommend getting some food down you folks. The snow is set to come on again after sundown. We can't be wasting any of the resources we have at the house. Anything that isn't eaten here, I shall feed to Jet and the cattle."

James replied evenly. "We aren't children, Allan. If we aren't hungry, we won't eat."

"A statement which sounds remarkably childish in the circumstances," he retorted.

Helen sighed deeply. "Come on, we need to remain positive and united. There was a nasty near miss today and we should be grateful everyone is okay."

"Some of us didn't get missed," Sasha said lightly, touching her hand to the gauze taped firmly to her forehead.

"How is it feeling?" Helen asked gently.

"The cut is starting to throb, but my headache has eased, thanks to the painkillers you gave me."

"I'll keep changing the dressing every few hours. I may need to give you antibiotics, but we'll wait and see. I've got some tetracycline in a thermos compartment in my medical bag." Allan swallowed a spoonful of soup.

"Did you manage to contact the doctor in Inverlael?" Dani asked.

"Yes, I finally got Dr Huntley on his home number. He's been busy visiting patients door-to-door, he still can't get his car out in the snow. He concurred with my choice of treatment. Obviously, he would like to see Sasha himself, but whilst that's not possible, we shall keep in close contact." He turned to his wife. "Mrs Huntley is going to check in on Andy this afternoon, make sure all is okay and he has enough provisions. Apparently, the local store is still well stocked. The local farms are delivering by foot or by sled."

Helen seemed relieved.

Tony finished the final slurp of his soup. Dotty had come down to join them, seeming in much better health. She was observing Sasha with avid curiosity, like she was an exhibit in a museum.

"I still can't believe you were hit by an axe," she said in her quiet, lilting tones. "You've been mighty lucky, mighty lucky indeed."

"None of us can quite believe it," Oliver added stonily. "It certainly wasn't in the entertainment plan."

Sasha nudged him gently. "Don't go on about it, love. It's not as if Uncle Bernie and Aunt Morag planned this. It was just an awful accident. Can't we forget about it and try to enjoy ourselves? We're still here to celebrate. If I can forget about it, I'm sure the rest of you can."

"What are we here to celebrate, exactly?" Dani asked innocently, amazed at the woman's stoicism, or stupidity.

"Oh, Uncle Bernie had some good news a few weeks back, something to do with clearing his name of a past injustice. He wanted to celebrate with all his oldest friends and family. Christmas seemed like a really good time to do it."

Dani wasn't convinced this random collection of individuals could possibly constitute Bernie's nearest and dearest. She and James certainly didn't fall into that category.

"Well, he didn't tell me about any such *celebration*," Allan stated. "If you'd asked me, I would have said the occasion was the anniversary of his and Morag's wedding. If I recall, it was on New Year's Eve five years ago. We hadn't met then, but he showed me the photos once, at dinner. It remained in my mind, because I thought it such an unusual date to get hitched, particularly in Scotland."

Sasha looked confused. "Yes, they did. I went with Mum. Morag wore a lovely velvet dress and the reception venue was all decorated like a winter wonderland. It was magical."

"If we are all here to celebrate with Bernie, how come he isn't with us now?" James dropped his cutlery with a clatter. "We are eating together and doing all these activities together, whilst Bernie is nowhere to be seen. He's less like a host and more like a hotel manager. And we are like his guests, lower-grade because we're not paying, guinea-pigs for a new money-making venture no-doubt." James pushed back his chair and stood up. "Whatever he told you to get you and your husband here," he said to Sasha. "I'm afraid was probably not true. We were led to believe there was going to be a grand, New Year Highland Ball. I have a funny feeling we've all been brought to this place under false pretences." He threw down his napkin and abruptly left the room, leaving his fellow guests in a stunned silence.

Chapter 22

The awkward atmosphere lasted a few more minutes before Dani got to her feet. "I'm sorry about that outburst, Sasha. This morning's events were a shock to all of us, and being stuck here on the estate means nerves are becoming frayed."

She waved her hand dismissively. "It's fine, I understand. It's hardly been the festive break we all expected. I'm beginning to wonder if we should have come at all. It's just my mum wanted me to develop a closer relationship with Bernie. My mum moved out when she was quite young to marry my dad and we've never had much to do with one another, so when the invitation came, well, she thought it was a good opportunity to build bridges." Her eyes pooled with tears. "But I've messed it all up by getting injured." Oliver wrapped his arms around her shoulders protectively.

"It's not *your* fault," Helen said. "If anything, you should be angry with your uncle and aunt. Much as I like Bernie and Morag, they should have taken better care of you, of all of us for that matter."

"How very *British*, you all are," Tony said with an uncharacteristically hard edge to his tone. "That axe nearly killed one of us. We should be asking Bernie and that groundsman of his some very serious questions. In fact, it may be time to call the police."

A rumble of disquiet spread around the table. "That's perhaps a little premature," Allan mumbled.

"You're on his payroll. You would say that." Tony stared at the vet with surprisingly piercing blue eyes.

"Hang on a minute," Allan puffed out his chest. "I tend to Bernie's herd from time to time, but I certainly wouldn't describe myself as 'in his pocket' as you seem to imply."

Dani raised her hand. "Calm down everyone. The last thing we need if we're going to be stranded here any longer is to fall out amongst ourselves. Actually, I agree with Tony. The police should be brought in to examine that target range, it's a bloody death trap."

Tony crossed his arms over his bird-like chest, looking smug.

"But there's no need to do that." Dani reached into her jeans pocket and brought out her warrant card. "I'm a Detective Chief Inspector with Police Scotland. I'm not on duty, but I can certainly file a report with my team back in Glasgow. I also called the local station when we got back from our walk to take their advice."

"I'm not surprised," Helen said firmly. "I knew you weren't a civilian when you dived in front of that axe to push Oliver out of the way."

"It makes sense now," Oliver muttered. "I really was lucky you were here."

"What did the local station suggest?" Allan had turned his attention fully towards Dani.

"They wanted to know how Sasha was. I told them her injury was relatively minor. The officer in charge wants to send out a squad car when the snow has cleared, to assess the equipment that caused the accident. He also wanted to know if Sasha or Daniel wished to press charges against Bernie."

Sasha looked shocked, as if the idea had never occurred to her. "Of course not! He's family!"

Oliver stayed silent.

"So that's it then?" Tony asked. "They're not even going to try and get an officer out here right now? What if we aren't safe?"

"There's nothing to suggest that's the case." As Dani spoke the words, she wasn't sure if she believed them herself. "But in the meantime I am here and if anyone has any concerns or wants to talk to me about anything, then please approach me privately."

Tony leant forward in his chair, his expression an odd sneer. "Does Bernie know you're a cop?"

Dani shook her head. "I don't know if James would have mentioned it to him. I was here as his partner, not for any other reason."

"Well, that's certainly interesting." Tony rapped his small fingers in the table as if to a tune none of the rest of them could hear.

"Now, if you'll excuse me and I'm going to go and check on James."

*

Dani found James in the library, pacing up and down in front of the lines of shelves, a glass of whisky in his hand. Jet was lying asleep in front of the fireplace.

"It's a bit early for that," Dani said quietly.

"I needed it. Today has been extremely stressful."

She placed her hand on his arm. "Please come and sit down. Tell me why you're so wound up. Is it something to do with the conversation you had with Bernie this morning?"

James dropped into the chesterfield armchair. "After breakfast, I wanted to have a word with Bernie, discuss some future work he might put my way. I came to find him in here. Morag said it was his favourite place to sit."

"Go on."

"I found him flicking through a building magazine. I used it as a way to introduce the topic of his business. I asked about his latest project and whether he'd had the legal side of it handled yet." James lifted his head and looked Dani in the eye.

"He started to laugh. He told me that men who hustled for business whilst on holiday disgusted him, especially when they were a guest in someone's home. His expression was mocking, pitying even."

"Oh, James."

"I was so shocked, I didn't know how to reply. In any other circumstance I would have come to find you, packed our bags and gone straight home, salvaged what we could of Christmas week. The man humiliated me." He gulped down a mouthful of whisky. "But we're stuck here, aren't we? Then that awful incident at the target range came straight after."

Dani perched on the arm of the chair. "I think you were right, about Bernie bringing us here under false pretences. He's playing with us. What he said to you, was to goad some kind of reaction. From what Tony was saying just now in the dining room, I don't think there's much love lost between him and Bernie either."

"Then why did the Shannahans come here? Dotty is clearly not enjoying herself one bit. They travelled a long way to visit a man they dislike."

"He must have something over them," Dani said quietly. "The only pair who genuinely seem friendly with the Ravens are Allan and Helen. When Sasha talked more openly, she suggested she barely had anything to do with Bernie. I think she's hardly seen him before this week, only briefly at weddings and funerals."

James narrowed his eyes thoughtfully. "Have they brought us all here for a particular reason?"

Dani jumped as a voice interrupted their whispered discussion.

It was Morag. "I just wanted to tell you that Mrs Noble is going ahead with the menu as planned this evening. She will be giving a masterclass on the preparation of the venison and chestnut purée in the kitchen at 5pm. There will be gin and tonics to accompany the lesson. We thought it might help take people's minds off the dreadful accident this morning. Sasha and Helen are definitely attending."

Dani nodded. "We'll see how we feel, thank you."

Morag seemed to hesitate for a moment, before slipping away. Dani glanced at her feet as she departed, gone were the four inch heels, replaced by a pair of velvety ballet flats. The detective thought it no wonder that this time when she approached, they hadn't heard her coming.

Chapter 23

The lights had flickered on in the department as the evening shift began. Dermot watched Sharon emerge from the lift; the teenager ambling along behind her was almost unrecognisable. His hair was clean and gelled and he wore a smart Nike tracksuit and shiny trainers.

The DI moved out from behind his desk to intercept them.

Sharon threw her jacket over the back of her chair. Jackson lowered himself into the seat opposite.

"Have you had a good day?" Dermot asked cautiously.

"Great!" Sharon replied. "We had turkey with all the trimmings for lunch, I decided to get the ingredients delivered, rather than bother with the mini-market. The DCS gave me a budget for Jackson, so I thought, who's going to care if we spend some at the sales on Buchanan Street?"

"The Fraud Office?"

Sharon laughed. "Jackson only had one set of clothes. We aren't allowed to return to the house yet, so I had to get some more. We actually picked up some excellent deals. You should take Serena down there."

Dermot ignored the shopping advice. "Well, I'm glad everything's going smoothly." He turned to Jackson. "Are you okay here for a while longer before I take you back to the flat? I've just got some work to finish up before I clock off."

"Sure," he added brightly. "I like it here."

"Could we have a word in the office?" Dermot asked his colleague.

"Is it confidential? Because it might interest Jackson to listen in on some police procedural talk. Good for his training." She winked at the boy.

Dermot sighed. "I suppose not. This isn't exactly official police business."

"Great, fire away."

"I had a call from DCI Bevan this afternoon."

Sharon sat up straighter in her seat. "How did she sound?"

"A little harassed, to be honest."

"Is that the lady who's up at Strathain House?"

Sharon nodded, "Yep, she's our boss."

Dermot tried not to look surprised at Jackson's knowledge. "There was an incident this morning at some kind of shooting range, one of the guests received a nasty gash to the head and another could've been seriously hurt."

"Were they using guns?"

"It wasn't entirely clear. The line wasn't great and Dani seemed in a hurry to finish the call."

"The estate was built as a hunting lodge originally. There would have been regular shooting parties taking place there a hundred years ago," Jackson added.

Sharon explained, "I've asked Jackson to do some research into the area for us, in case the DCI needs our help. It's purely from maps and the Internet. He's not using any of the official databases."

"Well, we may have to use some of those databases now."

Sharon furrowed her brow with interest.

"The DCI wants us to find out everything there is to know about Bernard Raven. He is the CEO of Raven Homes, the building company and owns Strathain House. He married his current wife, Morag on the 31st December 2016, but was likely married before. That's all the information she could give me."

"Well, it should be enough to be going on with," Sharon stated. "I can get Jackson to research the stuff in the public domain whilst I check out the Holmes database."

"Great, that sounds like a plan, and when you're ready to head home, Jackson, just give me the nod."

*

Dermot was settling back behind his desk when the extension rang. He picked it up, half expecting it to be Dani again from the Highlands.

"DI Muir? It's DCS Douglas here."

"Afternoon, Sir."

"I've had a call from the chief of police in Santa Cruz, Tenerife. According to the manager of the Hotel Europol, the Fleetwood family checked out two hours ago."

"Are they heading home?" Dermot's heartbeat increased its pace.

"The Reina-Sophia airport have the family's details, they will contact the British Consulate the minute the Fleetwoods produce their passports." Douglas paused, a silence stretching ominously on the line. Finally, "I don't think they're flying home. I've got a feeling they're going to do something silly; try and hide out from the authorities. Did you have any luck tracking down friends or relatives who have moved to the Canaries?"

"Not so far, They don't seem to have many friends in the UK, that I can tell. But I could ask Jackson, he's here with Sharon right now in the department?"

"Let's wait a few hours first. The family may walk onto a flight back to Prestwick and then our fears will be for nothing. As soon as we mention the situation to the boy, he's going to panic."

Dermot thought about the thirteen year old being told his parents and young siblings were potentially on the run from the authorities on a tiny volcanic island in the Atlantic and how disturbing that would be. "Yes, agreed. We only ask Jackson as an absolute last resort."

Chapter 24

As the light diminished in the sky outside the window of the drawing room, a steady fall of thick snowflakes began to settle upon the already white landscape. Behind her, Dani could hear Bernie setting the fire in the large grate.

She twisted round. "What kind of heating does Pete have at the lodge?"

Bernie straightened his back, prodding at the burgeoning flames. "The same as at the house. The generator heats his radiators and water. There's also a log-burner which I'm sure he's got lit. He's always chopping wood for it."

"Then I think he should come over to the main house with the rest of us."

Bernie opened his mouth to object.

Dani continued, "he'll be using diesel powered heating just for one person which will diminish your supplies. We've only got heating and lighting for as long as the diesel lasts. If he comes over here, it will keep us going for longer." She raised her eyebrows. "Unless you would rather the lights went out?"

Bernie laughed the comment off. "Of course not. I suppose you're right. With the weather closing in again, we need to conserve our resources. I'll get Mrs Noble to make up another room on the second floor."

"I'm sure Mrs Noble is busy with dinner and her *masterclass*. Pete can make up his own room, he can bring over his bedding from the lodge. James and I will go and tell him."

"Okay, but take good care out there in the fresh snow. Pete won't have had time to clear it yet."

"Don't worry, we'll be fine."

*

As Dani made her way to the staircase, Allan emerged from one of the downstairs rooms. "May I have a word?" He said in hushed tones.

Dani followed him into the library. The vet scanned the room, as if making sure they were completely alone. "I didn't tell the group everything about what Dr Huntley told me."

"Oh yes?"

"Sasha's wound is certainly not life-threatening and I'm confident there's no significant concussion, but Huntley confirmed what I'd been worried about myself." He shuffled from one foot to the other. "I taped the wound together as tightly as I could manage with the equipment I have here in my bag, but it should really have some stitches. It will heal eventually, of course, but without a hospital doing the job properly, there could be a nasty scar. She's only a young woman. The mark would be permanent."

Dani took a deep breath, feeling a wave of pity for Sasha. "Is there any possible way we could get her to the nearest hospital?"

"Well, the nearest hospital is in Inverness, so there's no hope of that, but there is a clinic in Ullapool which could at least stitch her up properly."

"How many miles is that?"

"About 15 miles. Huntley said it might be possible to get a four-by-four along the A835, but from here to Inverlael we'd have to trek on foot. That's about 5 miles."

"It wouldn't be possible now, not with darkness falling and the snow coming down."

"It also wasn't possible with Sasha in the state she was today; with a mild concussion and clearly in shock. I desperately don't wish the girl to be left permanently scarred, but keeping her alive is more important."

Dani felt a bubbling up of rage at the predicament they were in. Why had the Ravens insisted on involving them in their silly woodland expedition? "What should we do? You know this area better than the rest of us?"

"If the weather clears by morning, I'd like to try and take Sasha to the town."

"The snow will be even thicker by then."

"If we walk along the shore, at the banks of the loch, the snow won't have fallen as heavily there and we might get through. It will be one heck of a hike, but Huntley will be waiting for us at the other end."

"Okay, I think you should tell Sasha the whole truth and see what she thinks. If you both decide to go, you should take Pete Tredegar with you. He's meant to be the survival expert. I'm going to see him now, so I'll explain your plan."

"Good idea." He sighed heavily. "And I shall go and talk to Sasha."

*

The lights were blazing at the groundman's lodge as they approached along the path, trudging through the fresh fall of snow. Dani's chest tightened with irritation. Did he not know they needed to conserve the energy they had?

James knocked hard at the wooden door.

It took several minutes for Pete to answer. He was dressed in an old sweatshirt and jeans, thick walking socks on his feet. Heat blasted out of the cottage.

"Can we come in?" James demanded, his tone not inviting debate.

"Yeah, sure." Pete led them inside. The lodge was small but neatly designed with a galley kitchen off to the left and a sitting room making up the remainder of the ground floor.

Dani took a seat on a worn chintzy sofa in front of the woodburner which was pumping out a great deal of heat. "I've been talking to Bernie. We think with the weather deteriorating, it would be best if you moved up to the house for a few nights. Then we can conserve more diesel for the generator."

Pete remained standing. He was tall and broad, even without the padding of his outdoor gear. "My job is to be close to the forest, so I can collect the wood and keep the snow cleared."

"You can do that just as easily from the main house," James said impatiently. He hadn't taken a seat either. "We can't be heating an entire cottage for one person. It doesn't make any sense."

Pete rubbed his stubbly chin. "I suppose not."

"You can take one of the rooms on the second floor with the rest of us guests. Bring some bedding over and we'll find you somewhere to bunk up."

He glanced around at his cosy cottage reluctantly, but his shoulders dropped in resignation. "How are Sasha and Oliver?"

Dani proceeded to explain to Pete the fears Allan had about permanent scarring. She explained his plan to trek to the nearest town as soon as the weather changed.

"Of course I'll go with them. I've got some equipment we can use in my shed. But we'll be out of contact with the rest of you. There isn't any mobile signal out there."

"You don't have a satellite phone?" James asked.

"No, we've never needed one. Even in the worst conditions we're fairly self-sufficient up here. I was planning to get one if we ever started getting paying guests at the house, but that was a plan for the future."

Yet again, Dani was reminded they were being treated like guinea pigs, not worthy of the safety precautions that would later be installed as standard. "We'll leave you to get packed up," she snapped.

Pete's expression was concerned. "Wait, there's something I need to tell you."

"What?" James glanced at Dani, worry creasing his forehead.

"I went back to the archery range this afternoon. I wasn't going to touch anything, as I know you think the police should see it. But I wanted to get it all locked up." He looked sheepish. "In all the chaos after the axe went off course, and in getting Sasha back to the house I had left everything open and unsecured."

Dani felt a feeling of dread prickling up the back of her neck.

"I wanted to get the equipment box padlocked like it normally is, only, when I counted up all the axes, even taking into the account the one that's buried in the back wall of the hut. One of them was missing."

"What??!" James spat the word out. "Why the hell are you only telling us this now?"

Pete became agitated. "I wanted to be absolutely sure and I didn't want to panic anybody."

Dani slowly got to her feet. "It's good that you told us now," she said levelly. "But this information stays between us, okay? Sasha needs to go and get that treatment and if Allan knows about the missing axe, he'll never leave his wife here. James and I will have to keep everyone safe whilst you're away. I don't know how we'll do it, but we'll just have to try."

Chapter 25

The food was delicious. Despite the worries churning through her mind, Dani couldn't help but enjoy the rich venison, complemented by the sweet, nutty chestnut purée and dark green, iron-rich spinach.

A French red wine accompanied the meal and James had got through his first glass with swift efficiency, whilst he eyed his fellow guests with ill-disguised suspicion.

Bernie sat at the head of the table, Morag to his right side. "Well, the week hasn't got off to the start I was envisaging, but here we all are, with no great harm done."

Allan looked down at his plate, obviously fighting the urge to contradict his host.

"And I think we can all agree this meal is an absolute triumph, for which we have to thank Mrs Noble and her two trainee chefs, Sasha and Helen." He raised his glass and the others felt compelled to do the same.

"Of course, we must thank Mother Nature for her bounty and you intrepid lot for collecting the goodies for our table."

Dani wasn't sure how much more of this bonhomie she could take. She glanced across at Pete, whom she had helped to move his stuff into a spare bedroom on the second floor a couple of hours earlier. They'd had to wipe a deep layer of dust from the surfaces and turn on the radiator, waiting for the old system to crank up the heat in this neglected corner of the house. The groundsman's expression was sombre. He concentrated on the meal in front of him, probably contemplating the expedition ahead of them in the morning and aware they would need to be well fed in order to reach Inverlael in the conditions which awaited them.

Sasha seemed relaxed and in good humour. She was sipping her wine and listening to her uncle contentedly. Dani decided Allan must not have told her about the urgency with which she would require further medical assistance. It made sense, the younger woman should probably be left to gain a good night's sleep first.

Dotty picked and prodded at her food. The venison she had eaten a few mouthfuls of and the spinach was gone, but the chestnut purée was untouched, as if the chestnuts themselves were tainted by the day's events.

"What else have you got planned for us, Bernie?" Tony's question had a resigned tone to it, as if there were a set number of ordeals they were all going to be compelled to overcome.

"Much depends on the weather, Tony. I had hoped to take a boat out on the loch to fish, but the jetty remains iced up. Perhaps I should have invested in some skis and a lift to take us up the glen!" If his comments were meant as a joke, nobody laughed.

Morag put down her wine glass. "Listen, I know that many of you are a little nervous about the conditions out there, but you have to remember this is the Highlands of Scotland. Winters like this are commonplace here."

"That explanation may work on your future American paying guests, but it's unlikely to convince us. We know what winter in Scotland is like. These conditions are treacherous even by our standards." James drained his second glass of wine with a flourish.

"Now, now James. My wife was only trying to keep everyone's spirits up. The last thing we need are harbingers of doom, ruining the holiday season for the rest of us." Bernie's expression seemed friendly, but his eyes were filled with fire.

Dani felt the anger bubbling up within her once again, but knew she shouldn't rise to Bernie's bait. She was sure he was watching them all, seeing how they responded to the predicament they were in. "I suggest that after the meal we all get an early night," she said firmly. "The snow is still coming down out there and I heard on the radio in Mrs Noble's kitchen that power lines may be out of action by the morning. In which case, the best course of action would be to stay together in one room tomorrow, to conserve heat. Which room has the biggest fireplace, Morag?"

"The main sitting room, I suppose. We do have a good selection of board games in the cupboard in there too."

"Right, then that is where we shall congregate after breakfast."

"You're a real girl guide, aren't you Dani?" Bernie said, a sneer in the upturn of his lip.

James stiffened in his seat. Dani reached out and placed a warning hand on his arm.

"I'm more than that, Bernie. A Detective Chief Inspector in the Scottish Police Service."

If Bernie was surprised to hear this information, he didn't show it. "Touché!" He cried, raising his glass in another toast.

Dani raised her glass and took a sip, the expensive wine burning her throat like acid.

Chapter 26

Jackson glanced up from the screen of his laptop. "The snow is due to ease off at about 5am in the Ullapool area. But there are already reports of a powerline out of action to the town of Achnasheen, and a covering of up to 10 inches, settling mostly on ice."

Sharon knitted her brow with concern. "I hope they have power at Strathain House. The place will become very cold very quickly without it. What are the daytime temperatures looking like?"

"Not much above 5 degrees. With not much more than 8 hours of sunlight during the day."

That meant very long, freezing cold nights. Sharon shivered, suddenly deeply grateful for the department's often oppressively over-efficient heating system.

"I've looked up Bernard Raven on our criminal database," Sharon explained. "This will tell us if he has ever committed a criminal offence in the UK. Also, because of our shared system with Europe, it should inform us of any convictions over there. I cannot find any entries for him or his wife, which means they are clean."

"I googled Bernard Raven and his company. Two years ago they won an 'innovation in building' award for a development they built in Dundee, they won another one for an estate to the east of Glasgow not long after they started operating. Most of the results on an internet search of his name show newspaper reports about his building projects. Only one report was critical about him. Raven Homes built an estate in the borders where locals claimed the building company had promised to add amenities like a primary school and parade of shops which 5 years on had never materialised. The local paper ran a piece about it."

"Could you send that article to me? To be honest, it doesn't sound like Raven Homes are using tactics that aren't employed by pretty much every construction company in the UK. They promise the earth when all they really want to do is build houses cheaply and flog them for a huge price."

Jackson looked up from the screen of his computer and narrowed his eyes. "Our courtyard of houses on Clyde Wharf were only built a couple of years ago. My parents bought it off the plan. I have a funny feeling the construction company were called Raven. But I couldn't swear to it."

Sharon didn't really want Jackson to be thinking too much of that house, or about his parents. This was supposed to be a distraction exercise. But her curiosity was piqued none-the-less. "Why don't you look it up? The information should be online."

"Yeah, I will. And I can ask Dad when they get home. He really moaned about the sale, apparently there was loads of stuff they promised to throw in as part of the price that they never did. The solicitors had to get involved."

Sharon didn't reply. She had no idea when Jackson's parents might materialise. She'd had an e-mail from Dermot earlier. The Fleetwoods had not arrived at Reina Sophia airport yet. It was looking likely they were hiding out somewhere, which felt like madness. Yes, they were likely to be prosecuted when they returned home. The kids may end up in temporary care, but there was no evidence of long-term neglect or abuse. Despite being arseholes, their children were still better off with these parents than in the care system, as long as Child Services kept a close eye on them.

Sharon leant back in her seat and stretched her fingers until the knuckles cracked. Maybe there was more to this than they realised. Perhaps the Fleetwoods were frightened about more than the child neglect charge. Steve Fleetwood was a mechanic for a BMW dealership. It was a decent job, but surely didn't pay enough for the family to afford a townhouse on a luxury development like Clyde Wharf. She was itching to ask Jackson more about his parents; their spending habits and who came and went from the house. Perhaps her cop's instinct was stronger in the end than her nurturing one. Her thoughts were interrupted as Dermot approached their workstation, pulling on his woollen coat.

"Come on Jackson, time to go back to the flat and turn in."

The boy looked disappointed, but he pushed back the chair and got to his feet. "I've sent you an e-mail with that article attached. I'll see you in the morning, yeah?"

"Yeah," Sharon said with a smile. "You certainly will. Now, make sure you come off that X-box when Dermot tells you."

The two detectives briefly made eye-contact, both of them colouring slightly at the implication of Sharon's request, the suggestion it made of she and Dermot as the mum and dad and Jackson their son.

Dermot quickly turned his head and ushered the boy towards the lift. "Come on, let's get going. I've stayed later than I meant to as it is."

Chapter 27

As soon as the fires in the grates reduced to a few smouldering embers, the temperature in the house dropped dramatically. Dani had helped Mrs Noble to fill a dozen hot water bottles for the guests to take up to bed with them the previous night. Some were so old and smelling of perished rubber they reminded her of her grandmother's house back in Wales in the 70s and 80s.

Dani had spent the night curled under the heavy covers with James, trying to conserve as much body heat as possible. She managed maybe a few hours of sleep. James seemed to do better, his breathing steady and thick for most of the night. She suspected the wine had helped knock him out.

As for her, Dani was pre-occupied with the idea of someone in the house having taken and hidden the missing axe. It could be somewhere here, within the walls of the old castle. She had quietly suggested to the other guests that they lock their door whilst they slept. She didn't elaborate as to why, so they had looked at her with odd, disbelieving expressions.

So the night's sleep had been fitful, as Dani listened out for footsteps along the creaking floorboards of the corridor outside. At least most of them were gathered on the same floor of the house. There was safety in numbers. They needed to stick together.

When her phone alarm buzzed at 6am it was still dark outside. The hours of daylight at this time of year were desperately short in the Highlands. Dani forced herself out of bed into the freezing cold room. She shivered as soon as her bare feet touched the chilled floor. Pulling on her clothes with haste, she finally felt her body beginning to warm up. A hot bowl of porridge would help. She'd asked Mrs Noble to make some for breakfast, leaving the ingredients out by the range cooker in preparation the night before.

Dani turned the key in the lock and slipped out of the door. She went first to the Baxters' room, Allan opened the door immediately, as if he had heard her approach. He ushered her in. Helen was sitting on the side of the bed, still in her nightdress.

"I woke Sasha half an hour ago and told her and Oliver about my plan. She was very reluctant to leave Strathain. I'm sure she thought my concerns about scarring were unfounded, that I was making too much of it. But Oliver was very concerned, he persuaded his wife to make the trek. In fact, it was all I could do to stop him coming with us."

"Did you tell him he'd just be a liability? That if he succumbed to the cold or conditions Sasha wouldn't reach the medical help she needed?"

"Yes, I did. In the end, he agreed to stay here. I said we'd need him to be in the rescue party if any of us got into difficulties."

Helen had wrapped her arms around her body. "I'm not sure I'm happy about you going either, Allan."

He rested his hand on her shoulder tenderly. "I know that route better than anybody here. I've lived in the area man and boy. I will carry on with Sasha and Huntley when we reach Inverlael. Jean Huntley has been checking on Andy. I don't want you to worry. I'm going to leave my medical equipment here. If anyone needs painkillers or treatment for minor injuries, Helen can administer it. She's watched me enough times with the animals. But keep the bag locked, and carry the key on your person at all times. There are dangerous drugs in there."

Dani felt a pang of guilt. Allan was being so solicitous in making sure his wife didn't worry about his safety, yet Dani hadn't shared with him the information about the axe. He was leaving Helen in this house with someone who may well be capable of deadly sabotage, someone who could move onto something even worse. She would just have to make sure she kept the woman safe in his absence.

"If you make sure Pete and Sasha are dressed and ready, I will go down to the kitchen and make your porridge. Pete assures me he has energy bars and water in his backpack for your journey, but you'll need something hot and sustaining inside you before you leave."

Allan nodded sombrely, taking his orders without demur.

*

Dani left the kitchen as she found it. After the porridge had been consumed, she rinsed and washed the large, cast iron pot, setting it back on its hook beside the range.

The sun was only just beginning to rise behind the hills when the four of them trudged through the thick snow to the storehouse next to Pete's cottage.

"I've got flashlights and a pick-axe, in case we need to break the ice around the loch at any point. I also have a map of the route and some supplies."

Dani looked at Sasha, she was dressed in her thick padded jacket, waterproof trousers and walking boots. Her bandage was just visible beneath a thermal hat pulled down low over her head. "Are you okay for this?" She asked her.

Sasha nodded. "Yes, Oliver says I must reach the clinic and get myself properly sorted out. But I'm a bit nervous, I don't do much walking, especially not in hills like this."

Dani squeezed her arm. "You'll be fine, you are young and fit with expert helpers with you."

Pete nodded. "Yes, we should be fine as long as we maintain a steady pace. I will take Sasha and Allan to Inverlael and then return here before sundown."

Dani thought about the shortness of the days at this time of year. "Are you certain you can make it there and back before darkness falls? Do you have any way of alerting us if you get into trouble?"

"If we keep up the pace, I should manage to get back before dark. I've got some flares in my pack. Keep an eye out to the north. If we get into trouble, I will release a flare out over the loch."

Dani nodded. It was time to let them go. She shook Allan's hand and they exchanged a look that spoke volumes. Allan was to make sure this expedition succeeded and Dani was to ensure Helen was alive and well when he got back.

Chapter 28

When the rest of the guests came down to breakfast, there were three empty places. Dani filled her plate in silence, making sure she had plenty of protein in the form of eggs and bacon. James did the same.

It was Tony who eventually asked the question. "Where are Allan and Sasha this morning? Having a lie-in I suppose?"

Helen shot a glance at Dani. It was time to explain what was going on.

Dani put down her knife. She explained to those left at the table who had not yet been informed, of Allan, Sasha and Pete's expedition to Inverlael, to seek medical treatment for Sasha's head injury.

Dotty dropped her cup in its saucer with a clatter. "Why are they allowed to leave and we aren't!?"

Dani thought this was an odd way of phrasing it. "It won't be an easy journey for them. The main road is closed and the snow is knee-deep in places, they're having to circumnavigate the loch, which is also frozen solid. The temperature won't go above 5 degrees. The reality is that nobody should attempt it unless there is an emergency."

Tony nodded his head thoughtfully. "And you don't think there's any kind of emergency situation here, in this house?"

Dani again got the feeling Tony knew something the rest of them didn't. Perhaps he knew about the missing axe and where it was?

"No, I don't," she replied with a confidence she didn't really possess. "The weather should lift in the next few days, the forecast was much more encouraging today. There shouldn't be any further snowfall."

"But the stuff that fell last night isn't going to thaw anytime soon in these temperatures, is it? Not with the sun going down at 3.30pm?" Oliver hadn't touched his breakfast and seemed like he was worried sick about his wife, his face was pallid and drawn.

"You're right. But we need to be positive about the fact conditions won't be getting any worse. In the meantime, we should try to stay in the main drawing room today. We'll keep the fire lit in there and conserve the diesel that powers the generator."

"What do we do when that runs out!?" Dotty's voice held a hint of hysteria.

"That's the point of conserving the energy," James added gently. "The diesel should then last until the roads re-open. The council will be getting a snow plough along it as soon as they're able."

Dotty turned her piercing gaze towards Helen. "What if someone falls ill? I've already got a bad chill. Your husband was the only medically trained person in the house. Now he's gone."

"He was only a bloody *vet*," Tony muttered stonily.

"Allan has left me his medical bag," Helen explained. "If you need any painkillers, anti-inflammatories, or even antibiotics, then just come to me."

Dotty seemed placated by this offer.

Oliver raised his head. "What about sleeping tablets to help us at night. I know I need my energy but I just can't seem to drop off in this place."

"Well, all we have are animal tranquilizers and I really don't recommend taking those. Besides, we will need you alert and ready in case the expedition party get into difficulties."

Oliver dropped his head again, as if deflated by this news.

Dani stood. Let's get these plates cleared away and into the kitchen. I'll wash and Oliver and Tony can dry. James is going to collect wood from Pete's store. Then I suggest we congregate in the drawing room at nine and await our hosts.

*

Dani could hear Bernie's booming voice from her position at the kitchen sink. Someone had clearly told them about the departure of two of their guests along with the groundsman. Morag's voice was muted and calm, as if trying to smooth out the situation.

She shook her hands free of suds and padded to the doorway, where she could hear better. The couple seemed to be standing by the bottom of the stairs.

"Tony says they slipped out under cover of darkness," Bernie was railing. "None of them said a bloody word, not even at dinner last night. Well, it's insufferably rude, that's what it is. Throwing our generosity and hospitality back in our faces."

"Tony said Sasha needs proper treatment. She needs that wound properly stitched and a course of antibiotics, not just the ones you give to a dog or a cat. Who knows what germs were on the end of that axe, sitting in an old rusty box out there in the woods. The girl's your *niece*, Bernie. Imagine what Justine would say if we sent her home disfigured, for God's sake."

Bernie appeared to take a deep breath, considering his wife's words. "Okay, I can understand that. But why the hell didn't they tell us? I could have gone with them. Not to mention Pete Tredegar. He's my employee and he's taken off without a word. Well, when he gets back here he won't have a job to return to. I'll make sure all the estates in the Highlands know how unreliable and flaky he is, allowing someone to sabotage his equipment like that. Bloody amateur."

Dani listened to the heated exchange. She wondered how serious he was about sacking Pete, or if he was just letting off steam. Perhaps they'd been wrong to keep the Ravens in the dark? Although, deep in her gut, Dani felt sure that if they'd revealed their plans ahead of time, the expedition would not have taken place.

She stepped out of the shadows and confronted them. "Good morning. I hope you both slept well? James has set a fire in the drawing room. We are going to gather in there for the rest of the morning."

"Morning, Dani. It's interesting to see how after only a few days you're treating this place as your own. Almost as if you're the lady of the manor. I suppose that's a sign we've made you all feel very at home here." Bernie's eyes burned into hers.

She smiled at the sly comment. "You said there were some board games in there?" She directed her words to Morag.

"Oh yes, of course I'll show you."

Dani followed her hostess into the drawing room, where the others had all gathered around a roaring fire. Dotty had produced a knitting bag and was seated on the sofa, clacking away with the needles.

Morag knelt down and opened the door of an antique sideboard. She pulled out a pile of games; Scrabble, Monopoly and chess were amongst them, along with a pack of cards.

"Thank you," Dani said warmly.

"There's a card table over there, too. If you pull down the sides, you'll see it has a baize cover underneath."

James identified the table and went to open it up.

"Just place it by the window, darling. Then we'll have plenty of light to play by," Dani suggested.

She pulled across four chairs. Helen and Oliver automatically moved across the room to take their places. Dani made sure her seat was facing towards the window, angled in the direction of the northern tip of the loch. She imagined this was a position she would be taking up for most of the remainder of the day.

Chapter 29

The showroom was in darkness. Sharon put her face to the glass and examined the bank of executive cars in the forecourt. "Were these the kinds of cars you drove in the diplomatic service?"

"Yep," Dermot replied, standing a few feet back and taking in the whole of the glass fronted building. "Mostly the BMW 3 series or the Mercedes E Class. They are the vehicles of choice for diplomats and politicians. Jaguars are popular amongst patriotic types, especially now they're made by a British company again."

Sharon hadn't been expecting a lecture on the executive car market. She tapped the screen of her phone. "They're on reduced opening times this week, but the assistant manager is going to let us in."

On cue, a middle aged man in a shiny suit approached the entrance doors. He pushed the buttons on an elaborate looking security system which allowed the automatic doors to slide open. The officers showed their warrant cards.

"Thanks for making time to meet with us Mr Shaw," Sharon said.

He led them to a comfortable, modern office facing the showroom. "Not a problem, I'm working on the sales figures this week even though we aren't open to the public." He gestured to the seats on the opposite side of his desk. "What can I help you with?"

"It's a delicate matter, Mr Shaw, regarding one of your mechanics. We hope that our conversation here will remain just between us, as his case is still ongoing."

"Of course, now I'm intrigued."

Sharon continued. "You have an employee here by the name of Steve Fleetwood?"

"Yes, he's been with us for a long time, over ten years I believe."

"He is currently on holiday in Tenerife with his family, they are due to return home on the 1st January?"

Shaw reached for a large desk diary and began flicking through the pages. "Most of our technical staff take leave over the Christmas period as it's the quietest time for us. We do a lot of corporate rentals and they all stop after Christmas Day. We may get a handful of requests for the New Year but a skeleton staff can cover it." His finger traced across the page. "Correct, Steve is off until the 2nd January. I believe they're celebrating his 50th birthday whilst they're away. Is there a problem?"

Dermot cleared his throat. "We have a warrant for the arrest of Mr and Mrs Fleetwood when they arrive back on UK soil. Unfortunately, they have checked out of their hotel in Tenerife and we don't currently know where they are."

Shaw's mouth dropped open. "What are they being arrested for?"

"Child Neglect. It came to our attention that their thirteen year old son, Jackson, had been left in the house on his own whilst they were away. The couple are unlikely to receive a custodial sentence for the crime, so we are a little surprised they've not returned to the UK immediately."

Shaw rubbed his smooth chin. "I'm shocked. Steve has always seemed like a devoted family man. He's a quiet worker and very efficient. We've never had any problems with him."

"Were you aware the Fleetwood family had recently moved into a townhouse on one of the gated Clyde Wharf developments?"

"I knew they'd moved. He took a day off to get unpacked. But I didn't know the type of property." His expression displayed surprise.

"Does Steve earn enough from his job here to be able to afford such a property?" Dermot eyed the man closely.

"Well, the simple answer is no. Steve is on a basic mechanic's wage. But I do not know his wider circumstances; they may have inherited money or been helped out by a relative. It is a free country and I wouldn't pry into my employees lives in such a way as to question it."

Dermot nodded. "Yes, I agree. But Liz works as a receptionist part-time. Their wages alone could not have funded this move. We have gained access to their joint account. The mortgage on the property seems way below the market rate, which suggests a considerable down payment was made on the house at purchase. No record of such a payment exists in any bank account in their names."

"Someone else may have paid the deposit direct to the seller?" Shaw suggested. "We have that happen here quite regularly, when a parent or grandparent is contributing to the purchase of a car."

"Yes, that's entirely possible. Although, their closest living relative is Liz's mother, currently residing in a care home in Largs which is being funded by the sale of her bungalow in Saltcoats."

"I see. Then the cost of the property does appear to be a mystery. But not one I can solve."

Dermot shuffled up straighter in his seat. "Are there any ways that your staff can make extra money through the business here?"

Shaw furrowed his brow. "Not really. The mechanics are here to service the cars and get them ready for customers to collect. We don't need to get them to do overtime for that. Those here at the branch with the highest salaries are the sales and rental staff who work on commission, along with myself and the manager, who also work on sales. But Steve has never shown an interest in moving into that area of the business."

"Do you know of anywhere Steve and his family may have gone in order to avoid the authorities in the Canary Islands? Did he have any friends who have retired or work out there?"

Shaw shrugged his shoulders. "I didn't know him well enough to be party to information like that. To be honest I'm shocked by this news." He rubbed his eyes vigorously, as if trying to shake out some ideas. "The only person I can think for you to contact is Harry Price. He's another of the mechanics and he and Steve seem like good mates. Other than that, I'm at a loss."

Dermot and Sharon got to their feet. "If you can provide us with his contact details we would be most grateful."

"Of course." Shaw hesitated for a moment. "Should I be looking to find another mechanic? Only, if Steve doesn't come back, it will really leave us in the lurch."

Sharon sighed. "We have no idea, Mr Shaw. But as soon as we know more, you'll be the first person we'll inform."

*

They sat in the car, watching the sleet turn to icy water as it slid down the windscreen.

"I think he helped us as much as he could. I sense Steve is a valued employee. This recent behaviour has come from out of the blue as far as his boss is concerned."

"I agree." Dermot nodded. "But often, when a crime like child neglect is uncovered, it's the tip of the iceberg. You find that people capable of illegal behaviour will not just be committing one crime but several."

"Yes, that's true. It's fairly clear that Fleetwood is getting money from somewhere other than his pay packet. But there's no evidence of it going through his bank accounts."

"No, maybe we're talking about cash transactions. But we didn't find anything at the house when we searched."

Sharon shifted round in her seat. "Perhaps the burglars found it! They made off with the cash!"

"It's possible, but I don't think I'd hide the money at home, not if other members of the family didn't know I was involved in illegal activities. We found no trace of drugs either."

"Do you think Jackson knows anything about this?"

The muscles around Dermot's mouth tightened. "I don't think so, but we should really be questioning him about it."

"The DCS is babysitting him right now at the station. He may already be asking those questions."

"We don't have much time before we're going to have to undermine the lad's faith in his parents even further, perhaps fundamentally."

"Until then, let's get hold of this Harry Price chap and see if we can't get the information we need from him instead."

Chapter 30

A bright, winter sun was shining high above the hills. It was hard to imagine the temperature could be as low as it was outside of the house. But Dani knew the warm glow was deceptive. She glanced at her watch, they had four hours of daylight remaining.

The loch was perfectly still, the water a sparkling amber. There had been no sign of a flare and she'd been watching assiduously for most of the morning, with James keeping an eye out when she couldn't. Dani hoped the group had reached Inverlael by now. There hadn't been a telephone call yet to confirm they'd arrived and met Dr Huntley, but they may not have had the time to make it.

Dani put down her hand of cards and nudged James's arm, to indicate he should continue manning the lookout. She exited the drawing room and made her way up the stairs, hoping to be able to reach Bernie's study without interruption.

She heard a creak on the stair behind her. Dani spun round, her heart beating fast. Helen was standing on the step below, her face a mask of worry.

"I need to show you something," she said in hushed tones. "Come to my room."

Dani allowed Helen to overtake her and followed in her wake. When they reached the Baxters' bedroom, she closed the door firmly behind them.

"Do you think Allan has got Sasha to Inverlael yet?"

"I was just about to use the phone in Bernie's office to find out. Allan left me Dr Huntley's number so I thought I'd call. They may not have the opportunity to inform us."

"Good idea." Helen knelt on the rug by the double bed and pulled out her husband's medical bag from underneath. She rummaged in the pocket of her tweed jacket for the key and opened it. "I thought I'd do an inventory of items after breakfast this morning, just so that I know what's in here in case we need it."

"That sounds sensible."

"Allan has a notebook he keeps in the back which lists the drugs and equipment he has at any one time. You have to be very careful in his profession." Helen opened the bag wide and showed Dani the neatly packed contents of drug packets, phials and un-used syringes and dressings. "There are some painkillers gone and a roll of bandage and several gauze dressings which were used for Sasha's injuries. Allan hadn't had chance to cross those off the list, but I found something else missing that I can't account for."

Dani lowered herself onto the bed. "What is it?"

"There should be three packets of prednisolone, which is a form of steroid used for allergies in dogs. There are only two in here."

"Maybe Allan prescribed the tablets and forgot to cross it off his list too?"

"Well, it's possible but unlikely. My husband is meticulous with his paperwork, especially with drugs like steroids which can be abused in the wrong hands."

"There's not much missing though, is there? I've worked enough on drug cases to know that a month's supply of 5mg dog steroids wouldn't be worth much to an addict or a dealer."

"No, it certainly wouldn't. But I was thinking about Jet the other day, when he was barking so viciously at Sasha and Oliver at the foot of the stairs. It was so out of character, you see. He's usually such a friendly, passive dog."

Dani shook her head in frustration. "I don't understand. What has that got to do with anything?"

"Well, one of the side-effects of taking prednisolone in some dogs, especially if given in a higher than normal dose, is abnormally aggressive behaviour."

Dani took a few moments to consider this. "Do you think someone gave Jet this drug to make him aggressive? Maybe the Ravens' dog needs to take the steroid for a legitimate reason?"

"No, Jet has been on our books since he was pup, he doesn't suffer from any allergies. We would never prescribe him prednisolone tablets."

"Could someone have taken the tablets from Allan's bag and then given them to Jet? That would have been a couple of days ago. I thought Allan always kept his bag locked?"

"He does and a couple of days ago it was locked in the boot of our Land Rover too. But Allan was here the day before Christmas Eve, dealing with a bull that was lame. He would have been in the barn with his bag open. In those circumstances, anyone could have passed by and taken something from it. If Allan was treating the animal, he'd be unlikely to notice. Then it was Christmas and we were all so busy; cooking, wrapping and getting ready for this visit."

Dani crinkled her brow. "So who could have had easy access to the bag?"

"Well, the obvious culprit would have been Pete or Bernie, but I suppose either Morag or Mrs Noble could also have come into the barn if they wanted to."

"Then they have to be our main suspects. But why drug your own dog? Why make him more aggressive? It doesn't make any sense?"

"The aggression will only last until the drug wears off. I suppose if you were trying to frighten someone, or warn them off, then it could be something you would do, but it's pretty heartless to use an animal in such a way."

"It was Sasha and Oliver who were on the receiving end of that aggression. Was someone trying to frighten them particularly?"

"And it was *their* target which got sabotaged on the shooting range. Although, I don't see how the person doing the sabotaging could possibly know where our groups were going to stand."

"If you wish to manipulate people into standing in a certain position, there are certainly subtle ways of doing it. Especially if you are the one running the show." Dani gazed out of the window at the leaden, grey sky and shivered. She got to her feet. "Let's see if we can make that phone call shall we?"

The women walked softly across the carpeted landing. The door to Bernie's office was ajar. Dani pushed it gently, relieved to see the room was empty. She tip-toed towards the mahogany desk and lifted the receiver carefully. Her expression knitted with concern. She jabbed at the switch hook and followed the coiled cord to the connector on the wall where it was still firmly plugged in.

"What's the matter?" Helen's voice was tremulous with fear.

Dani let the receiver fall back into its cradle with a thud. "I'm so sorry Helen, but the line is dead."

Chapter 31

When they returned to the drawing room, Dani tried to keep her tone light. "Shall I make a pot of tea for us all? Would anyone prefer coffee?"

Dani made a mental note of the orders of her fellow guests. She looked towards Morag and Bernie, who were reading at opposite ends of one of the worn Howard and Son sofas, Jet lying asleep by their feet. "Morag, could you help me in the kitchen, please?"

When they were out of earshot, Dani said. "I tried to ring Dr Huntley's surgery from Bernie's office. The phone line is dead."

Morag put a hand to her delicate throat. She seemed genuinely surprised. "Are you sure? Why would it be?"

"The telephone line could have come down in last night's snow. We'd have to check with BT. But we've no way of contacting them," Dani added through gritted teeth.

They entered the kitchen. Morag asked her housekeeper to heat some water on the range. She invited Dani to sit with her at the table. "The box containing the telephone connector is on the side of the main house. We could always open it up and have a look?"

"That might not be a bad idea. At least then we'll know what we are dealing with." She lowered her voice. "Helen thinks some drugs are missing from Allan's medical bag. Do you have any idea who may have taken them?" She couldn't be certain, but the detective thought she noticed a flicker of disquiet pass across Morag's chestnut brown eyes.

"No, I don't. What kinds of drugs do you mean?"

"A steroid for dogs. It treats allergies and works as an immune suppressant, but in the right doses, can make an animal highly aggressive."

She shrugged her narrow shoulders. "I really don't have a clue." Her vision shifted to the kettle on the stove, getting to her feet. "Let me find the tea and coffee pots, Mrs N. We can make up a tray."

Dani got the distinct impression her hostess didn't want to discuss this issue any further. "Did anyone notify Sasha's parents about her accident, before the phone went out of action?"

"Yes, I believe Sasha called herself after it happened, although she kept the details brief. There was no point in distressing Justine more than was necessary. There is only my sister-in-law, her husband died a couple of years ago."

"I'm sorry to hear that."

"He'd been in a wheelchair for a while. An accident at work left him with awful back trouble."

"Was Sasha their only daughter?"

"Yes, Cliff wasn't very well after she was born, I'm not sure they could have managed with another."

Dani took a breath. "And what about you and Bernie? Do you have any children, from previous marriages, perhaps?"

A bloom rose to colour Morag's cheeks. "I don't have any, no. But Bernie has a son and a daughter, from his first marriage."

"Do they live in Scotland?" Dani wondered why neither of them were spending Christmas at the house with their father.

Morag shifted from one foot to the other, seeming distinctly uncomfortable. She kept glancing nervously at the door, as if someone might walk in and find her discussing things she shouldn't be. "Oh, they're both very grown up now, living here and there. Very busy these younger people, aren't they?"

Dani nodded, noting her vagueness with interest. She realised Sasha could probably have told her more about these cousins, but now she was gone. Perhaps Oliver knew something about them?

Morag and Mrs Noble filled the pots and got together a selection of cups and saucers. Dani opened the large fridge to look for milk. Her eyes slid down to the bottom shelves where several bottles of Moët champagne were stacked up on their sides. Perhaps these were for their New Year celebrations? Although the idea of celebrating now seemed distinctly odd.

"The Baxters mentioned it was your wedding anniversary on New Year's Eve?" Dani shut the door and poured the milk in a jug.

Morag snatched the jug from the table, placing it on the tray with a clatter, as if she were tired of Dani's questions. "Yes, it's our fifth anniversary. We were hoping for a lovely celebration on the 31st, but the weather and then that awful accident with the axe, has ruined those plans."

To her surprise, Dani saw tears gathering in Morag's eyes. Mrs Noble moved silently across the room and placed her arm around her boss's shoulders. "Now, now, Mrs Raven. I'm still going to make you a lovely meal for your celebration, don't you worry."

"Do you have family you need to contact, Mrs Noble? They must be worried about you, stuck out here in this weather?"

The housekeeper jerked her head up and fixed Dani with a hostile stare. "I live here. The Ravens are my family."

Morag brushed off the older woman's embrace and gripped the handles of the tray tightly. "Honestly, so many questions. Has anyone ever told you that badgering people for information is really quite rude?"

Dani picked up the other tray, ready to follow her host out of the door and back to the others. "Oh yes, Morag. Many, many times."

Chapter 32

Harry Price lived in a grey stone terraced house in Govanhill. Dermot decided this was a much more likely property for someone on a mechanic's wages to occupy.

Price answered the door to the detective and stood back to allow him inside. The hallway led to a deceptively spacious front sitting room with a Christmas tree positioned in the bay, facing out onto the street.

"My wife's taken the kids to her mother's. They're only in Partick, but my mother-in-law's giving them some lunch, their cousins are going too." Price sat on the sofa, beside a discarded Partick Thistle scarf.

Dermot perched on the edge of an armchair. "As I explained on the phone, I'm here about Steve Fleetwood."

Price nodded resignedly. "Aye, you said they'd not come back from their holiday. Left the older kiddie at home?" He shook his head sadly. "I don't know why they didn't ask Katie and me to have the lad. We've not much room, but he could have shared with Dougie, they're much the same age."

"You and Steve are good friends then?"

Price pursed his lips, his muscular frame stiffening. "We've worked together for ten years. We talk about our wives and kids, the price of petrol and all that, maybe have the occasional pint after work, but I wouldn't say we were *friends*, exactly."

"If I did all that stuff with somebody, I would consider them a friend."

"Not if that person looked down on you and yours you wouldn't."

Dermot raised his eyebrows, waiting for the man to continue.

"Steve moved in different circles to me. Even when they lived on the new estate round the corner. Their place was *detached*, you see?" Price sighed, "they were always going on these swanky holidays with the kids. Cyprus one year and Tenerife the next. My missus was always askin' where the money came from. I said it was none of our business. Then they moved into that new place on Clyde Wharf. It was all brand new and easy to look up what one of the houses cost. I nearly spat out ma' tea when I saw the figure."

Dermot couldn't help but smile. "How do you think the Fleetwoods were affording this lifestyle?"

"Well, it wasn't for me to ask, but we were always speculating. We thought they'd had a win on the pools or something, a scratch card, maybe. Kept it on the quiet."

Dermot maintained a neutral expression. "Did you ever suspect the money came from activities that were illegal?"

He dropped his head, examining his calloused hands intently. "My missus certainly did."

"What about at work? Could Steve have been taking private clients? Servicing cars out of hours?"

Price raised his head. "I did consider that. I also thought maybe he was chauffeuring on the quiet. A lot of our clients provide transport for top officials. He could easily have been doing nights for cash-in-hand. It's something our bosses didn't like. They pay us a decent enough wage, we're not expected to moonlight on the side."

"But it wouldn't be illegal to do that, for extra money?" Dermot thought this a definite possibility. He knew himself how many parties and official engagements these dignitaries attended back when he was providing security for them.

"No, it wouldn't. But he'd still have to do a heck of a lot of driving to make the kind of money that house was costing."

"True, but that was the market cost. Maybe Steve knew the builder and was able to negotiate a better deal?"

"That development was Raven Homes wasn't it? They've got a reputation for being hard bastards. I knew someone who laid bricks for them on a development. Long hours and rubbish pay, he said. The big boss was ruthless. Used zero hours contracts and sacked you for a sick day. Can't see him dropping a couple of noughts from the cost of one of his houses, can you?"

Dermot couldn't. He'd already done some research into Bernard Raven and he was a hard businessman. The man whose estate Dani was currently staying in had certainly trodden on a few toes on his meteoric way to the top. "Okay, thanks for talking to me. Just one more thing. Do you know of anyone in Tenerife the family could have gone to stay with? An ex-colleague who has retired out there, something like that?"

"Nope. But one of the sales people could well have a place out there, they're the ones who make four figure commissions. But I don't know any of them well enough to say for sure." Price got to his feet. "Where is Jackson now? Is he okay?"

"Yes, he's fine. We've found him temporary foster care and I can personally vouch for him being well looked after."

"Good. Otherwise me and Katie would have him. If you could tell the social services people that, I'd be grateful. We don't want him ending up in one of those kiddie's homes."

"I will, thank you." Dermot made his way to the door.

"The only other thing that struck me about Steve," Price abruptly added, "was always how attentive he was in his work."

"How do you mean?" Dermot stood still.

"Well, if he was working on a car, getting it ready for a client, he was almost obsessive about making sure he handled everything himself. He'd do the safety checks and all the valeting. Like it was his own little project. I learnt to leave him to it over the years. I tried a couple of times to help with the finishing off, or do a sight test on one of his mechanical jobs, but I soon learnt to stop. He got quite shirty about it. So I left him to it. When you work with someone for all those years, you learn their funny ways, tolerating them is the only way to get by."

Dermot absorbed the man's words, saying nothing. He nodded his gratitude again and headed out to the car, his mind full of thoughts.

Chapter 33

The wind had picked up and it was bitterly cold. Even with gloves on, Dani was struggling to hold the screwdriver to loosen the screws on the BT box attached to the brickwork on the north side of Strathain House.

Oliver was kneeling beside her. "Here, let me have a go. The screws are iced over. I'll need to chip some off to get a purchase."

"Does that mean it's not been touched in a while?"

Oliver shrugged. "Not necessarily. In these temperatures I'm sure it could ice up in a few hours. The sun doesn't reach this side of the house."

"I'm sorry we haven't been able to get in contact with Sasha. But nobody has set off the emergency flare, so we've got to assume they got to Inverlael okay."

"I certainly hope so. When is Pete due back? He should be able to tell us."

Dani tipped her head up to the sky. The sun was beginning to slip below the distant hills. "He needs to be back before dark. Unless he decided to stay in the town until tomorrow because of the walking conditions. We've no way of knowing now if he changed his plan."

Oliver sighed in frustration. "I wish we'd never come here. I don't know why Sasha was so keen. We're in the middle of nowhere and she hardly knows Bernie."

"I think that was the point. Sasha wanted to establish a better relationship with her uncle."

"I love her to bits, but my wife is too much of an idealist. From what I've seen, Bernie isn't much worth the effort."

Dani couldn't help but agree. "Does Sasha have anything to do with her cousins? Morag said Bernie has two children from his previous marriage."

"Nope, I think she met them when she was very young but that was it. Of course, they sided with their mother in the divorce, which was pretty unpleasant by all accounts. They never really moved into Bernie's new life. They refused to take the name for a start, thought it was ridiculous, as did Sasha's mum. Bit of an insult to their dead parents, you know?"

Dani rested back on her haunches. "What do you mean by, 'take the name'?"

Oliver paused from his task to look at her. "Didn't you realise? Raven isn't Bernie's *real* surname. He took it on when he established the new building business. Must have thought it sounded more dynamic, interesting. His kids kept their old name. I'm not surprised, bloody odd thing to do in my opinion."

"So what was his name before? What was Sasha's mum's maiden name?" Dani's face was numb with cold, she could barely get the words out.

Oliver had to crinkle his brow in concentration. "I'm fairly sure it was Corder. When Sasha first mentioned him to me, he was plain old Bernie Corder. Now he's Bernard Raven, the multi-millionaire CEO."

Dani felt a stab of frustration. If they had an operational phone, she could have called Dermot and told him. They wouldn't get very far with their research if they only had the name 'Raven' as a reference point.

Oliver grunted as the last screw finally came loose. He eased off the casing and they both peered inside.

Dani gritted her teeth against the chill and the confirmation of her worst suspicions. The telephone line lay in two parts, having been cut neatly in half.

Oliver rested his head in his hands. "Oh shit," he muttered darkly. "Just what the hell is going on here?"

Chapter 34

When the sun dipped below the hills, darkness followed swiftly. The house was abruptly cast in gloom; shadowy corners stretched out to make the furniture just a dark outline and the features of its occupants veiled and indecipherable.

Dani and Oliver had shed their outdoor gear and were standing in front of the fire in the drawing room, trying to warm their frozen limbs in the heat from the dancing flames. Oliver's forehead was etched with worry.

James moved across from the window to join them. "No sign of a flare over the loch," he informed them. "But no sign of Pete returning either and daylight is fading fast."

"We have to assume they reached the town. We would have heard something otherwise." Dani lowered her voice. "The phone line has been deliberately cut."

James jolted, as if receiving an electric shock. "Who would do that? Why?"

Oliver rubbed his hands together vigorously. "I'm glad Sasha is safely out of here. I've been beside myself with worry all day thinking about that journey, but it turns out she's better off than the rest of us."

"I think we should keep this to ourselves for now." Dani glanced at the doorway to make sure they were alone.

James gave her a puzzled look.

"We don't know who cut the wire, so letting that person know we are aware of what they're up to makes us vulnerable. Also, it's best not to cause panic."

Oliver nodded reluctantly. "But it had to be someone who knew where the external telephone box was. That's got to rule out the Shannahans and probably Helen as well."

Dani shrugged her shoulders. "I don't think it would be difficult to find it if you really wanted to. But it would have to be somebody who could open that box in the freezing cold. I can't imagine Dotty managing that. But I don't think we can rule out the possibility it was one of the group who left this morning. It could have been done before they set off."

"Well, it wasn't Sasha. She was with me the whole time."

They turned their heads as footsteps approached. "You look like conspirators hatching a dastardly plan." Bernie entered the room with Jet at his heels. "Morag has decided to light candles around the ground floor, to conserve electricity. We plan to serve dinner in the dining room as usual. I was hoping James could help me light the fire?"

"Of course." James's tone was without enthusiasm.

"No sign of Pete yet?" Bernie glanced out of the bay window where the last of the light was fading fast.

Dani couldn't tell if their host seemed concerned about his groundsman or not. "No, not yet. And we can't check they arrived safely as the phone is out of order."

"Yes, there must be a telephone wire down between us and Inverlael."

Oliver raised an eyebrow but said nothing.

"I bet Pete has decided to cut his losses and stay in the town. He can hardly come back here after taking off without even so much as having the courtesy to tell me."

Dani felt anger flare in her chest. "I certainly believe he was planning to come back. All his possessions are at the lodge and he wanted to help us."

Bernie took a step forward. "Do you think you need *help*, eh? Well, it's looking less and less like that's going to arrive, doesn't it?"

James stepped between them. "Let's go and light that fire, shall we? There are still plenty of logs in Pete's store room."

Bernie turned and swept from the room, the draught caused by his exit nearly snuffing out what remained of the flames in the grate.

*

None of them seemed to have much of an appetite. Mrs Noble had done her very best to produce a good meal. They had watercress soup followed by pan-fried salmon and potato dauphinoise. The housekeeper had told Dani earlier that the freezer was full of vegetables and meat. They also had several four litre bottles of milk in there, so she had plenty of options for meals when added to her pantry ingredients.

It had almost felt to Dani that someone had been anticipating being cut off from the outside world for a lengthy period. It was like a paranoid catastrophist preparing for the apocalypse.

Conversation was stilted. The Shannahans seemed to have given up entirely on polite discourse. Tony had eyed his dinner companions with undisguised suspicion as he sipped his soup. Dotty looked a bundle of nerves.

Helen's posture was stiff and the pursing of her lips revealed the worry that was eating away at her regarding the whereabouts of her husband. But she still managed to exchange some words with Morag about the changes they were planning for the formal gardens at the front of the house.

Bernie sat at the head of the table, seemingly oblivious to the shambles his house party had descended into. He merely gulped his French Bordeaux appreciatively, is if he hadn't a care in the world.

James had clasped Dani's hand underneath the table. She worried for a moment that her boyfriend was actually shaking, but then his arm rested comfortably along the length of her thigh.

"I'm sure Mrs Noble could eat with the rest of us," Oliver commented, his tone barely civil. "It must be lonely for her out in the kitchen. I thought we were supposed to be sticking together?"

Morag glanced up from her salmon. "Oh, Mrs N will be doing some jobs before she sits down herself to eat. But don't worry, it all stays perfectly warm in the range."

Oliver was clearly about to say more about this inequitable state of affairs when a loud bang resounded through the house, shaking the window at the far end of the dining room. He jumped to his feet.

Dotty dropped her knife and fork with a clatter and began whimpering, Tony placed his arm around her shoulders.

"What the hell was that?" James cried, now out of his seat.

"It came from outside," Helen added levelly, she was clearly someone who remained calm in a crisis.

Dani pushed back her chair and tried to think carefully. "Oh my God," she announced suddenly.

"That was one of the emergency flares. Someone must have set it off outside!"

"What?" Bernie seemed genuinely baffled. "Why would they do that? If it's Tredegar, he must be nearly back so why would he need a distress flare?"

"Perhaps he's injured," Morag added worriedly. "He could easily have fallen or twisted an ankle in the dark."

Just as they were about to rush from the room to investigate, Mrs Noble came dashing in from the kitchen. "I was washing the soup pan and I saw a bright flash in the sky. There was an explosion and I thought the window would come in on me!"

"Show us," Dani ordered, allowing the woman to lead them back into her domestic domain.

She stopped at the window above the butler sink and pointed, whilst the others gathered round and looked. "The flash of light came from out there, right in the middle of the woods."

Chapter 35

DCS Douglas gazed out of the window of the office at the lad tapping feverishly away on the computer on Sharon's desk. "I'm not sure how much longer we can keep from the boy the fact his family have gone on the run."

"Not much longer, Sir. I agree. But my conversation with Steve Fleetwood's colleague at the garage was very interesting. He doesn't know about anyone who might be living in Spain, but he had certainly noticed the Fleetwoods' spending habits far outstripped his wages."

"So, he was on the make in some capacity. Now we are arresting him and his wife for child neglect, he most likely thinks we are onto him for whatever else he's been up to. Unfortunately, we aren't."

Dermot ran a hand through his hair, sending it up on end in tufts. "I've been onto the management company who sold the house in Clyde Wharf to Steve and Liz Fleetwood. They referred me to their solicitor. The person who handled the sale is currently on leave for Christmas, won't be back until next week."

"You say it was a Raven Homes development and this Raven CEO is the man Dani and James are staying with in Ullapool? Why don't we try and have a word with him, get him to encourage his staff to cooperate with us? If he's friends with James, that might be our way in?"

Dermot hesitated, then decided to tell the DCS about Dani's whispered phone call and her request to have them do some digging into Bernie Raven's past.

"Why didn't you tell me this earlier? Are they in any danger up there? Get Dani on the line!"

"I can't. The phone line has been out of service for the last 12 hours. I've reported it to BT but they haven't got back to me yet with an answer. The engineer I first spoke to said a lot of their lines are down in the bad weather and I should just be patient."

"What about on her mobile for heaven's sake?" He looked at Dermot's troubled face. "There's no signal is there? Wi-Fi?"

Dermot shook his head dolefully.

"Then I'll get onto the local station, see if they can get an officer out to the house. Give me the damned address at least."

"I'll e-mail it to you now, Sir."

Douglas left the office door swinging open behind him as he strode away, not uttering another word.

When the DCS had got into the lift, Sharon padded across the office floor and popped her head round the door. "Everything okay?"

Dermot sighed. "You might as well come in."

Sharon took a chair. "The DCS looked pissed off."

"He was. I told him about the situation with the boss up at Strathain House. I thought now that Bernard Raven had a connection, albeit a loose one, to our case down here, he ought to know."

"And he wasn't happy we hadn't told him earlier?"

"Not at all."

"Well, Jackson hasn't found much more out about Raven and his wife. The business has only been around for about 15 years and before it was founded, we can't find anything out at all about Bernard Raven. No birth certificate, first marriage certificate, driving registration, nothing."

"What about his wife?" Dermot leant forward with interest.

"I located their marriage certificate. They had a civil ceremony at Hanslow Hall on 31st December 2016."

"That's out towards Motherwell. Serena and I had a tour of the place, but it was really out of our budget, just Serena dreaming big."

"Morag Raven was previously Morag Jennifer Linsdale. She grew up in a comfortable, middle-class home in Dumfries. Her father was a history lecturer who took up property development on a small scale later in his career. I reckon that's how Morag's path may have crossed with Bernard's. But before Raven Housing was established, it's as if her husband never even existed."

"Shit. What are we missing here, Sharon?"

"I don't know. But I could always give Mrs and Mrs Linsdale a call? They are quite elderly now, but I got a number for them from Mr Linsdale's driving license details. I'm sure I could ask a few innocent questions about their son-in-law?"

Dermot rubbed his tired eyes. "I don't know, Sharon. We've got absolutely no jurisdiction to be investigating the guy. This couple could report us to the DCC."

"If I'm careful, it shouldn't come to that." Sharon leant forward in her seat. "Dani's up there in that house, cut off from help. Now the phone line is dead, I say we can step up our investigation. If something happens to the boss, we won't forgive ourselves if we don't try everything."

"You're right," he sighed deeply. "I wish you weren't, but you'd better go ahead and call them. Let's just hope we don't regret it."

Chapter 36

"Why would Pete set off a flare in the woods? It isn't even on his route back from Inverlael?" Bernie was pacing the flagstone floor of the kitchen.

"I don't know, but we need to go and investigate," Oliver said firmly, the hint of a waver in his voice. "Sasha could be out there! She might be in trouble!"

"But I thought Sasha and Allan were going on to Ullapool?" Morag said evenly.

"That was the plan," Helen snapped. "But we have no idea whether they ever got there safely. Not now the phone line is dead!" The woman finally lost her composure and allowed the tears forming in her eyes to slide unchecked down her cheeks.

Morag placed her arm around her friend's shoulders. "I'm sorry. I know you're worried about Allan. But I really don't think he can be out there. It must be Pete."

Dani stepped back from the window, from where she'd been gazing out into the darkness, trying to make out some movement in the trees beyond the house. She'd seen none. "We can't be sure of anything right now. But a group of us will have to go out and investigate where the flare originated. I suggest that James, Oliver and I go. Bernie and Morag stay here with the rest of the guests."

"It's my bloody estate! Don't tell me what to do!" Bernie boomed.

"You can come with us if you really want," Dani continued. "But we need people here in case Pete manages to make it to the house. There's safety in numbers. I think the fewer of us going out into the cold and dark the better."

Bernie seemed to begrudgingly agree. "Okay. You're going to need flashlights. There are some in the utility room."

"Right," Dani said with authority. "Let's get ourselves fully kitted out."

*

As soon as they stepped out of the kitchen door, the bitterly cold air hit them like a wave on a stormy beach. Dani pulled her hat further down over her head and pointed her torch towards the trees.

"Should we really be leaving the rest of them alone in the house?" James said when they were a few metres from the back door. He was thinking of the missing axe and where it might be.

"It's not ideal, but what choice do we have?"

"Do you really think the others back there are in danger?" Oliver said.

"I don't know," Dani said truthfully. Right now she wasn't sure if the danger was coming from outside, from the wilderness they were heading straight into. but she didn't mention this to Oliver.

"We don't have an exact location for where the flare was set off. If we keep two metres apart and sweep the immediate area around us we will still be within calling distance of one another. We need to be in constant contact. Nobody is going to get lost out there." As they reached the line of trees, Dani took a deep breath and led them inside the thick wood.

The snow thinned out underfoot and the trees were acting as a barrier to the wind, but the depth of the absolute darkness beyond the narrow beam of their flashlights was terrifying. The sharp smell of pine filled Dani's nostrils along with one of dampness and decaying wood.

As they walked further into the forest, Dani began calling out for Pete. Then, she heard her two companions doing the same, like an eerie echo.

The beams of their torches formed criss-cross patterns on the forest floor. They were looking for signs of anyone having been there; footprints amongst the pine-needles, broken branches. If Dani had had her work team and sufficient back-up, they could have used heat-seeking technology to find if anyone was alive and injured out there. Although, the density of the trees would still have made the job difficult.

They were walking deeper into the trees, the gradient rising gradually, indicating they were heading up the glen. Dani knew from the maps how large this forest was. There was no way they could cover the entire area themselves. Yet, the flare had seemed so close to the house.

"Over here!" Oliver's voice rang out around the trees.

James moved across to join Dani and they wove through the narrow trunks until they spotted Oliver's stationary light. "Hey, there's something here!"

Dani jogged closer, directing her beam around Oliver's feet. She spotted the abandoned flare casing lying between two gnarled roots protruding from the ground. "We shouldn't touch it," she said.

James began striding around the surrounding area, shouting Pete's name. He returned a few moments later, shaking his head. "There's no sign of anybody. Surely if you set off a distress flare, you stay close to it and wait for help to arrive?"

Dani felt a growing sense of unease. "Pete would certainly know to do that, wouldn't he?"

They heard a snapping of branches a few metres ahead of them. Dani pointed her torchlight into the blackness. She saw nothing but trees and shadows.

"What the hell was that?" Oliver hissed. "If it's one of the others, why aren't they calling out to us?"

"It could have been an animal." But Dani wasn't convinced by her own words. This forest was too dense and dark for much to grow, it therefore wasn't particularly attractive to wildlife.

"I think we need to head back to the house," James said warily.

Dani knew her boyfriend wasn't saying this because he was frightened for himself, but because he was forming a similar idea to her. That the setting of the flare had been a diversion, a way of getting them away from the house and leaving those inside more vulnerable, without their protection.

"Yes, you're right. We'll leave the casing here for when the local police can come. There's no sign of Pete or the others out here. Let's track our way back the way we came, and this time, we up the pace."

Chapter 37

Dermot had come out to check on Jackson, leaving Sharon to make the call to the Linsdales from her mobile in his office, with the door firmly shut. She had insisted on using her own private number rather than the DI's extension. If this call came back to haunt them, Sharon was willing to take the fall.

Jackson had made copious notes on a pad beside the department laptop which had had its police databases locked by the IT department to be safe for his personal use.

Dermot picked up the pad. "Is this all stuff about Bernard Raven?"

"Yep," Jackson spun round on his chair. "It's mostly about Raven Homes. All their accounts are available online through the Companies House website. All I needed to do was create a login."

"Okay, did you find out anything interesting?"

"Well, the business was only founded in 2006. Bernard Raven is listed at the sole company director. But they took on some big projects right from the very beginning. There was a housing estate in Burnt Mills, Lanarkshire which was completed in 2009. It brought in a gross profit of 10 million pounds."

Dermot whistled through his teeth.

"But that had to be taxed and then used for wages. The company has about 30 permanent employees and then the labourers are employed if and when they're needed."

"Zero hour contracts."

"Yeah, that's right, it's the way many industries are choosing to plug their labour gaps."

"Because they can get away with it. How come you can interpret all that data so easily?"

"I'm studying Business Studies for my Highers. They like us to look up real-life companies on the internet and assess how they are doing."

"Oh well, it's come in useful already."

"I could even piece together some information about the development where I live, on Clyde Wharf."

Dermot felt a stab of guilt that they hadn't shared with the boy the latest information they had about his parents. "What did you find out?"

"Well, I read all the online brochures and looked up the costs and profits for the year it was completed and the last unit sold, which was 2019. It seems that development brought in nearly 20 million in gross profit. Mainly because Raven Homes was able to buy up the land cheaply as it was run down and used to be part of the old docks. But the company marketed the area as really up and coming which meant they could charge more. Although, having lived there, I don't know how much that's true. I see plenty of dodgy people along the riverbank path behind us smoking pot and doing deals."

Dermot made a mental note to inform Vice. "But all you need is for buyers to believe it's up and coming in enough numbers, then the house prices start to rise."

"Yeah, that's how it works. Places once seen as no-go become fashionable, like Cowcaddens. After the war, everyone wanted to move out of the city into the suburbs, away from the tenement slums. Now, the fashionable people want to be buy in the inner city, close to shops and bars. The tenements that are left have been done up and are highly desirable."

"Well, I'd award you the highest level in the subject if I was your examiner."

"I'm not sure my teacher would agree."

"Then there's something wrong with the education system." Dermot dropped into one of the swivel chairs. "So, this guy makes big money and he was producing award-winning housing estates within months of setting up Raven Homes. He must have been in his early 50s in 2006. To me, there's no way he was new to this business."

"There's no evidence Bernard Raven was involved in any construction companies before 2006, not according to Companies House, anyway. There's just no information about him at all before 2006 on the internet."

"Which is odd in itself."

"But not surprising," Sharon called over, as she walked towards them from the office. She flung her notebook onto the desk.

"Why not?" Jackson asked eagerly.

"What did they say?" Dermot found himself getting sucked up into the teenager's youthful enthusiasm.

"It was Mrs Linsdale who answered. I told her my name and rank, said I was making calls about home safety over the Christmas period; not leaving expensive gifts on show, have lights on a timer when visiting the relatives, that kind of thing."

The deception left Dermot feeling distinctly uncomfortable. But he couldn't deny Sharon got results. "Go on."

"It wasn't difficult to strike up a conversation about her family. She immediately complained that they certainly wouldn't be leaving the house empty this season as their daughter hadn't invited them to stay this Christmas, despite living in a Highland Castle with a dozen bedrooms. I displayed an interest in how she came to be living in such a grand place and Pam, which is Mrs Linsdale's first name, was only too willing to inform me her daughter was married to Bernard Raven, the owner of the well-known building company."

Dermot couldn't help but feel that rather than promoting personal safety, Sharon had been encouraging from this elderly lady the sort of disclosures they regularly told people to avoid telling cold callers at all costs, regardless of who the caller said they were on the phone.

Sharon must have noted his unease. "I had already told Pam never to give out her bank details over the phone, what she was telling me was general family stuff."

"What did she tell you about her son-in-law?!" Jackson cried out in frustration.

"When she mentioned Bernard, I commented on the name 'Raven', how I'd always found it so unusual and mysterious. Pam was very quick to tell me that of course, Raven was not his real name. Bernard had changed his name by deed poll to Raven only a few years before he met Morag. Pam and Johnny had been a little put out at Morag taking on the name when they married. Morag had been late to take a husband, so they'd got used to her being a Linsdale. Then, to take on a new name in her late forties, and one that wasn't even *real*, had caused them some upset."

"So what was his name before?" Dermot found he was holding his breath.

"Oh, she couldn't remember. Said they'd never even known him when he had his previous surname so it hadn't stuck in her memory. All she could recall was that it was something very ordinary." Sharon's eyes were bright. "But now we know it's not his real name, don't we? That's why we couldn't find any information about him before 2006. That's got to be something to be going along with, hasn't it? We certainly aren't going to waste any more time trying to find out about Bernard Raven before he changed his name, are we?"

Dermot tried to hide his disappointment. He hoped Sharon was right, because he had a funny feeling time might just already be running out.

Chapter 38

Helen Baxter had felt anxiety gripping her chest ever since Dani and the others had gone out to investigate the sending up of the flare. If the party that set out that morning from Strathain House really were in trouble, where on earth had they been for all these hours? How had they ended up in the woods when they'd headed off in quite the opposite direction at 6 o'clock that morning? What if they were injured? They must be, otherwise they'd have come straight to the house, surely?

She'd tried to remain in the drawing room with the others. Bernie and Morag were playing '21' at the card table. Dotty was knitting by the fire and Tony was staring at the pages of a crime novel, although she wasn't at all convinced he was actually reading it. He looked more like he was in a trance.

Only Jet was providing her with any comfort. He had come to lie by her feet and she petted him behind the ears. It never ceased to amaze her how animals could always tell when a person needed their support and calming presence. Although, she felt her anxiety must have been palpable to anyone within a mile of her right now, it didn't require the enhanced senses canines possessed. The clammy hands, heart palpitations and sweat prickling her brow were dead giveaways.

Finally, Helen could take it no longer. She got to her feet. "I'm going to fetch a glass of water. Would anyone else like one?"

The others shook their heads silently, all seemingly intent on what they were doing, although Helen thought they could not possibly be. She left the room and entered the kitchen, where Mrs Noble was still stacking dishes into the dishwasher in the utility room. She couldn't face a conversation, so took a glass from a cupboard and filled it at the sink, staring out into the darkness, hoping to see a sign that Dani was on her way back. There was nothing. She couldn't even make out the edge of the trees.

Helen went out into the hallway and climbed the stairs. On the second floor she headed to the room she'd shared with her husband up until today. A lump formed in her throat. She sat wearily on the edge of the bed and took her toiletry bag from the top drawer of the bedside cabinet. She popped out a 5mg tablet of diazepam from a packet languishing at the bottom and washed it down with a glug of the water. She wouldn't usually take them, but this situation was an emergency. For Allan and Andy's sake she couldn't allow herself to become a bag of nerves, unable to think straight.

She checked under the bed to make sure the medical bag was secure and exited the room quietly. Helen reached the top of the stairs and grabbed the handrail for support, she suddenly felt dizzy with the stressful events of the last couple of days. As she closed her eyes for a second, trying to steady herself, her body abruptly jolted forwards as a force hit her back, directly between the shoulder blades.

Helen felt the heavy glass slip from her fingers and bounce down the wooden steps ahead of her. For a few moments, it was like she had taken flight; like the soaring buzzards they saw regularly on their walks through the glen.

The flying sensation ended as her body hit the floor of the first landing. She felt bones snapping and her head hitting something hard and unyielding. Then, nothing but blackness.

*

Voices were beginning to enter Helen's consciousness. Something cold was touching her forehead and her eyes flicked open.

"She's waking up!" Morag continued to dab at Helen's brow with a damp kitchen towel. The blood that had a few minutes ago been dripping from a wound to her scalp had now begun to dry up. But Morag was concerned about the unnatural angle at which her friend's leg was bent underneath her. She knew the pain would hit soon, once the shock subsided.

Helen looked around her. She saw a sea of faces. "Somebody pushed me," she croaked.

Morag leant closer. "What do you mean?"

"I was pushed," Helen managed with a stronger voice.

"Are you absolutely certain?" Bernie demanded.

"Yes, I bloody am." She tried to shift her position. The pain shot through her body like an injected drug. Helen cried out.

"Try not to move," Morag urged. "I think you've broken your leg. Bernie and I will carry you. It's going to hurt, but we'll find you some painkillers, I promise."

Helen gritted her teeth hard as her two hosts lifted her weight gently and moved her towards the drawing room, where they set her down on the sofa. The pain in her leg was almost unbearable. She remembered giving birth to Andy at the hospital in Inverness seventeen years earlier. It'd been a busy night and they were low on nitrous oxide, so she couldn't even have gas and air. If she'd got through that, she'd get through this.

"I'll find some painkillers for you," Bernie shouted, as if it was her ears that were broken.

"There's some in Allan's medical bag," Helen said weakly. "The key is in my pocket."

Morag plunged her hand into the pockets of Helen's woollen jacket, one after the other. "It's not there, Helen. It must have fallen out when you fell. We'll go and check."

The pair left the room before Helen had a chance to reply. The truth was beginning to dawn. The push down the stairs, the time she'd spent unconscious. There seemed little doubt to her that they wouldn't find the key on the stairs, or in the hallway either. It was gone. The person who had shoved her without a moment's hesitation, had undoubtedly taken it.

Chapter 39

They spoke in lowered tones out in the hallway.

Dani had left her boots in the utility room and was standing in her thick socks on the parquet, wringing her hands to get some warmth back into them. "Is the leg definitely broken?"

"I'm no doctor," Bernie said, some of the bravado knocked out of him by the sight of Helen's injuries. "But I'd say so. The bone was at a terrible angle, but it hadn't punctured the skin."

"I'm going to make a splint for her," Morag explained. I'll just need a thin piece of wood and some bandages."

"There must be some in Allan's medical bag," James offered.

The couple shot one another worried glances.

"What is it?" Dani felt the dread she'd experienced out in the woods return once more.

"The key for the bag is no longer in Helen's pocket. We've checked up and down the stairs. There's no sign of it. We went into Allan and Helen's room and checked under the bed. The bag has gone too."

Dani sighed heavily. "Shit. Whomever pushed Helen down the stairs, wanted the key to that medical bag and access to the contents. They struck whilst James, Oliver and I were out on a fool's errand following that flare. The idea was to divide the group, weaken us."

"Do you think the same person who set the flare also pushed Helen down the stairs?" Morag looked perplexed. "How could they have managed it? We were all at dinner together when the flare went off?"

"Where was everyone when Helen was pushed down the stairs?" Oliver asked, his tone full of urgency.

Bernie creased his brow. "Helen had just gone out to get a glass of water, she said. It made me realise I fancied something stronger, so I went to the dining room to pour myself a whisky and Morag a brandy."

"And whilst Bernie was gone, I went into the kitchen to see if Mrs Noble needed any help. She wasn't in there, so I assumed she was seeing to the rooms upstairs."

"So Mrs Noble may have been on the second floor when Helen was attacked?" Oliver said eagerly.

"I don't know. You'd have to ask her."

Dani turned to the Shannahans, who were seated like statues on a chesterfield sofa against the far wall. "What about you two? Where were you after Helen left the drawing room? Did you see anything unusual?"

Dotty stared at her with milky eyes. "We didn't go anywhere. We stayed by the fire until we heard the terrible thump when Mrs Baxter fell, then we all congregated at the foot of the stairs. I thought she was dead, she was so still."

"We were together in the drawing room," Tony concurred. "Although, nobody else can confirm that, except the dog."

Bernie puffed air out of his cheeks. "I don't see how any of us would have had the time to get up the stairs ahead of Helen, hide and then give her a shove. None of us are spring chickens. But what about Tredegar? What's happened to him? He's got access to the house and was due back hours ago. If anyone was going to be setting off flares, it would be him, surely?"

Dani could certainly see the logic in that argument. "Come on, we need to make sure Helen is comfortable at least. Have you got any of your own medical supplies in the house?"

"I've got a packet of Naproxen left over from a back injury I had last year," Bernie offered.

"There's a medical kit in the pantry," Morag stated. "I just need to find something to use as a splint."

"There are some pine slats that came off one of the old beds upstairs," Bernie announced. "We could use one of those. We could always tear strips off a sheet to secure it to her leg."

"Good, you go and collect the stuff together. I'll sit with Helen until you get back." Dani turned on her heels and headed for the drawing room.

*

It was warm in the room with the thick curtains pulled across the draughty bay window and the fire crackling in the grate.

Helen was lying across one of the sofas with a blanket placed over her and a cushion under her head. Jet was lying on the floor beside her, whimpering in sympathy.

Dani pulled up one of the upholstered stools with a tassel fringe. The woman's face was deathly pale. Matted blood had congealed along her hairline.

Her eyes flickered open. "Allan. Did you find him?"

Dani shook her head. "We found the flare casing in the woods but there was nobody out there. I'm sorry."

"It doesn't make sense."

"No, it doesn't. How are you doing?"

"It hurts, my leg. The rest of me is numb. I took a diazepam just before I fell. At least I'm half asleep."

Dani smiled. "Bernie's got some painkillers, but we'll make sure we don't overdose you. Listen, once the drugs kick in, Morag is going to re-set your leg and strap you up."

She nodded, but her face paled even more. "It's going to hurt badly. I know. I've seen it done to many animals over the years. Sometimes the shock can be enough to kill them."

Dani found her hand and gripped it tightly. "We'll make sure you're dosed up first, I promise."

"There's a phial of morphine in Allan's bag?" Her tone was hopeful.

Dani said nothing.

"It's gone isn't it? The bastard who pushed me has got the bag."

"Yes. But we're going to find it. Helen, did you catch a glimpse of the person who pushed you? A shadow out of the corner of your eye as you approached the stairs, anything at all?"

"No, it happened too quickly. I had my eyes shut, I was feeling dizzy."

"It's okay."

"I'd been in the kitchen getting a glass of water. Mrs Noble was filling the dishwasher. I went upstairs and took a pill, then I walked to the top of the stairs."

"Mrs Noble was in the kitchen when you got your water?"

"Yes, I didn't feel like talking to her so I slipped in and out quietly."

"But she could have seen you in there?"

"I suppose so. She didn't say anything if she did."

"Okay. Try and rest now. Morag is going to come back with your pills and sit with you."

Helen's eyes closed and her breathing steadied.

Dani got up and quietly exited the room, pulling the door shut behind her.

James was standing on the other side. "How is she?"

"She's had a knock to the head which left her unconscious. She's undoubtedly got concussion so someone will have to watch her all night. But the leg break is the most concerning. There could be internal bleeding. Hopefully we can keep her comfortable for now, but we should to get her to hospital as soon as we can. We need the mountain rescue helicopter."

"It won't be flying in this weather and we've no way of contacting them." James's cheeks flushed red. "Who the hell would do this? What has Helen ever done to deserve to be left injured in this way?"

"I've no idea." She gripped his hand. "Now someone in the house has that medical bag. There's probably enough drugs in there to poison the whole of Inverlael."

"Good God." James pulled her to him and they shared a tight embrace. "I love you," he muttered in her ear.

Dani was about to reply when a noise jolted them apart. It was so unfamiliar, it took her a while to work out exactly what it was.

Someone was knocking at the large, wooden panelled front door.

Chapter 40

The BMW showroom was still closed. As Dermot peered in through the thick glass, amazingly polished clear of smears and smudges, he could see a light spilling from under one of the office doors. He hammered loudly, so that the panel shook.

Josh Shaw emerged into the showroom, a worried look on his face. When he recognised Dermot on the other side of the glass, his features relaxed. He punched in a security code and allowed the doors to glide open. "DI Muir, is everything okay?"

"Yes. Although there's still no word from the Fleetwoods."

The man ushered him inside. "We haven't heard from Steve either. As far as we are concerned, he's going to swan into the garage in 48 hrs time as if nothing has happened."

Dermot silently hoped that would be exactly what did happen. But experience told him otherwise. "I spoke to Harry Price. He seems like a good, loyal employee."

"Absolutely, we've never had any issues with his work. I'm going to call him today actually. If Steve isn't returning to work, we're going to need Harry to do some extra hours for us, take on greater responsibility. A promotion to chief mechanic might be in order. Good staff are hard to find."

"You're not wrong there." Dermot cleared his throat. "Harry had no idea if Steve knew anyone with a house out in Tenerife, but he mentioned that if anyone they knew from work did, it would be someone in the sales department."

"Well, we do earn more money than the technical staff do. These cars sell for high prices and we are on commission with our sales and rentals. Some of our team put their money into property, sure."

"Is there any chance you could find out if any of the properties are in the Canary Islands?"

Shaw shrugged. "I can call around. But I must assure you, Steve doesn't mix with the sales team. I've never known him to come out for drinks with us or even spend any time up here on the sales floor. He doesn't have a mate on my team."

"But there is some contact between the showroom staff and the garage?"

"Oh yes, if we need a quick turnaround on a sale, one of my team will go into the workshop and check how the mechanical checks are going."

"Well, if you could make those calls as soon as possible, I would be most grateful."

"Yeah, fine. I'll do it right now."

*

Sharon's flat was warm and smelt of floral air freshener. Jackson sat on a padded stool in front of the TV, explosions filling the screen as he navigated his way through Call of Duty. Headphones were fortuitously blanking out the accompanying noise, they were left only with the relentless flashing images.

Dermot accepted a cup of tea and relaxed into the soft cushions of the sofa, turning his head to the side to avoid succumbing to a seizure. "I'm waiting to hear back from Josh Shaw at the car showroom. It was a long shot anyway, I'm not expecting much."

"It's worth a try," Sharon replied. "We've got to tell Jackson the full truth soon. It could be that his family are never coming back to the UK."

"I still can't work out why. We found nothing incriminating when we searched their house after the break-in. We know Steve must be getting money from some illegal activity, but we've no idea what it could possibly be. So why abscond? The kids will start to ask questions. Liz will want to see her elderly mother and surely they'll all want to see Jackson again?"

Sharon sipped her drink. "I'm getting stonewalled by Raven Homes and their management company. We'll need a warrant to obtain any further information from them."

"We're lucky Steve's workmates are being so co-operative. It will be days yet before we get any forensics back on the burglary and odds on the perps were wearing gloves. Jackson reckons that path along the river is a regular meeting place for drug transactions. There's no CCTV and it leads out into an industrial estate which is a warren of alleyways."

"They could even have got away by boat."

"Yep, there are lots of abandoned barges down that way which would be an ideal store for stolen goods."

"We could get them searched?" Sharon looked hopeful.

"But we don't even know exactly what the robbers took, not until the Fleetwoods can confirm what's missing. Usually by now we'd have some descriptions of jewellery so we could at least go round the pawn shops on Anchor Street. It doesn't help they didn't take anything with a serial number like a telly or games console."

Sharon shifted round in her seat. "What if the point of the break-in wasn't to steal stuff?"

Dermot furrowed his brow. "What the hell else could have been the reason?"

Sharon drained her mug, thinking this over. "Perhaps it was to send a message, frighten the Fleetwoods. If Steve is getting money from illegal activities, then he must be involved with some nasty people."

Dermot glanced across at the boy, to make sure he wasn't listening. He seemed engrossed in tracking an enemy unit. "If that's the case, then Steve isn't frightened of us arresting them for child neglect when they return, he's frightened of someone else."

"Someone who could do far worse to them than unleashing social services on their backsides."

Dermot drummed his fingers on his thigh. "Price mentioned how meticulous and protective Steve was with the cars he serviced. He wouldn't allow anyone to check them over but him. He'd been that way for years."

"So what could he have been doing to them, some kind of sabotage?"

Dermot thought carefully. These vehicles were the type he'd driven for the five years he was in the diplomatic service. Shaw told them they were often rented out to important dignitaries for functions. These people had professional drivers to take them from place to place. The drivers were heavily vetted to ensure their backgrounds were squeaky clean as they were party to all sorts of confidential discussions. He'd learnt himself to tune out the things he heard at the wheel of these executive cars. Sometimes it was better not to know.

"What is it?" Sharon pressed.

"Those cars ferry around politicians and top business people. There would be certain organisations who might pay good money to find out what was said in them and where they were coming from and going to."

Sharon slowly nodded her head. "Steve could have been planting listening devices and trackers. As the mechanic, he could hide them in places nobody would think to look in a casual check."

"Not unless you were another mechanic."

"Could he really have got away with putting bugs in cars used by government officials, just like that? I mean, you would know how rigorous the checks would be?"

"Technology was changing all the time, even in the five years I did the job. In the months since I left I bet these GPS trackers could be the size of a pinhead. We swept all the vehicles of diplomats and ministers, sure, but I've no doubt we missed a fair few. Steve could have been placing them inside the body of the vehicle itself."

Sharon's eyes brightened. "This could be it, the answer we've been looking for!"

"We've got no proof, it's just theory. Certainly not enough to raise a warrant to search any of those cars Steve serviced. Even then, there's no guarantee we'll find anything, not if he's a pro."

"Then we keep looking. They always make mistakes, that's how we catch them. There'll be an email somewhere or a phone call to link him to criminal activity. We just have to find it."

"And find them." Dermot looked deflated.

Sharon rested her hands in her lap. "Have you got to get back?"

"Yeah, I should. Serena's still at her parents but I need to get a decent night's kip."

"Does she know about us looking after Jackson?"

Dermot hesitated before replying. "Not yet. I'm hoping he'll be settled with a foster family before she gets home."

"Okay, I get that. No need to worry her unnecessarily."

"Exactly."

"Do you want another cup of tea before you go?"

Dermot found he was comfortable where he was, buried in Sharon's overstuffed sofa. For the first time in days, he felt relaxed. "Yes, why not. One for the road can't hurt."

Chapter 41

The knock came again, more insistently this time. Mrs Noble brushed past Dani and James, heading towards the door.

"Hang on, please," Dani called out, recovering from her surprise. "Let me go, Mrs Noble. We don't know who it might be."

The housekeeper stood aside.

Dani wrenched open the heavy door. On the snow-covered step stood a man wrapped up in winter hiking gear. He was tall and had a woollen cap on his head and a pair of modern walking canes in both hands. The detective decided he was aged around forty.

"DCI Bevan?" He asked curiously. "I'm DC Duncan Hart from Highlands and Islands police, based at Inverlael. After we received your phone call the other day about the accident with the axe, my boss thought I should come over and check everything was okay."

The normality of this fellow officer's presence made the tightness in Dani's chest loosen a fraction. "Please, come in. How on earth did you get here? The roads are blocked and it's pitch black out there?"

The man stepped over the threshold, stamping his icy boots on the mat. He rested the poles in a wrought iron umbrella stand and reached for his warrant card, which he handed to Dani. "Actually, there's some moonlight over the loch, now the clouds have cleared. I followed the same route Mr Baxter took this morning. They'd cleared a decent enough path as they went, doing the hard work for me."

James took the man's damp coat and hung it over the newel post, ushering him towards the kitchen where the range cooker was providing some heat. "So Allan Baxter and his group reached Inverlael safely?" He asked.

DC Hart nodded. "Dr Huntley had informed us they were coming. I met them at the doctor's surgery at 1pm. They had a quick bite to eat and then set off in a Land Rover to Ullapool. I'm afraid I left before there was confirmation of their arrival at the clinic."

Dani dropped into a chair at the table. "That is a huge relief. We must tell Helen."

Mrs Noble had poured the officer a mug of tea from the pot warming on the stove. He took it gratefully.

"What about Pete Tredegar? He was meant to be coming back here tonight?" Dani enquired, eager for information after having been starved of it for so long.

"Mr Tredegar had slipped on some ice and twisted an ankle during the hike to Inverlael. He was not badly injured, but hobbling. The Doctor insisted he remain in the town until it healed up. He's bunking up with the Baxters' boy."

"Ah," Dani sighed. "That's why he hasn't come back." She immediately thought about the flare that had been set off in the woods behind the house. She told Hart all about the incident and about Helen's serious injuries after being pushed down the stairs in order to gain access to the medical bag.

The officer furrowed his brow deeply. "There's still too much snow to get an ambulance here and there's no way the helicopter can fly. But a paramedic team can get over here on foot. They will have the right drugs to keep Mrs Baxter comfortable until an ambulance can get through. I'll call them." He got out his mobile phone and stared at the screen. "Where is it best to find a signal?"

Dani's shoulders dropped. "There isn't one. The landline appears to have been cut and there isn't any Wi-Fi. We haven't been able to contact the outside world for two days."

Hart's expression was grave. "No wonder we couldn't get through when we called. I assumed the telephone pole had come down." He glanced around him, "where is everyone else? We're going to have to keep them together, especially if someone here has violent intentions."

"Morag and Bernie are with Helen in the drawing room. Oliver went upstairs to change out of his wet clothes and I assume the Shannahans went to their bedroom."

"Then bring them all back down. We don't want to disturb Mrs Baxter. Is there anywhere else we can congregate?"

"The library," Mrs Noble declared. "I'll go and set the fire."

"I'll come and help," James said.

*

Despite being advised against it, Bernie stood by the fireplace with a large glass of whisky in his hand. "So Tredegar is injured, is he? So much for the advanced survival skills he boasted about in his CV."

"I'm not sure that's fair, darling. Anyone can slip in icy conditions." Morag was seated in the chesterfield armchair.

Bernie rolled his eyes but said nothing.

Tony and Dotty sat in a pair of matching upright chairs in front of the bookshelves. Tony turned to DC Hart. "Can you get us out of here, officer? My wife hasn't been well since we arrived. I just want to get her home."

Hart gave him a sympathetic look. "I'm sorry, Mr Shannahan. As I'm sure DCI Bevan has told you, the roads remain impassable. But if your wife requires medical assistance she can be prioritised alongside Mrs Baxter when the paramedics get through."

Oliver grunted. "She's hardly in the same state as poor Helen. The woman has got a mild chill, that's all." He made eye contact with Hart. "Please tell me how my wife was when you saw her? How did she manage the hike over to Inverlael?"

"She was fine, Mr Preston. Mr Baxter had been guiding her the whole way and helping her through the ice and snow. Mrs Preston was in perfectly good spirits when they left for Ullapool."

Oliver's posture crumpled with relief. "Thank God. I've been imagining all sorts."

"Now, we need to focus on more serious matters." Hart nodded towards Dani.

The DCI continued. "Whilst we are all here together in the library, DC Hart is going to conduct a search of the house. Allan's medical bag is missing," she cleared her throat, "and Pete informed me before he left that one of the axes was missing from the store box at the target range."

Morag gasped.

"So we need to know if these items are still in the house," Dani finished.

Bernie took a slug of whisky. "Do you realise how big this place is? There are two upper floors with seven bedrooms on each, not to mention the old servants' quarters on the attic floor. Most of them remain unrenovated and are full of dust and old furniture. It would take hours for one man to search it all."

"Then I'd better get started," Hart said resignedly.

"Wouldn't it be better for two people to conduct the search?" Oliver said. "I'd do it."

"We're all suspects you idiot," Bernie rasped. "You can't be the one searching if you've hidden the thing in the first place."

"But I was outside with James and Dani when Helen was attacked. It couldn't possibly have been me!"

"But it could have been you who took the axe, couldn't it? Or you could have an accomplice who was in the house when you went out, establishing yourself an alibi." Bernie drained his glass, opening the cabinet beside him to locate the bottle.

"For pity's sake," Oliver muttered.

Dani held up her hand. "There's no point in fighting amongst ourselves. I expect that's exactly what somebody here wants us to do. But Bernie has a point about the size of the house. There are several outbuildings too, which could have been used to stash the bag or the weapon."

"What do you suggest?" Hart's expression was open.

"We start with the guests' bedrooms. I expect whoever took these items wants to keep them close to hand. They haven't got time to rummage around in attic rooms if they might happen to need them."

The room fell silent, as those occupying it imagined in what circumstances these items might be needed.

"Okay. That's a much better plan," Hart said firmly. "I'm leaving DCI Bevan in charge whilst I'm gone. She will check on Mrs Baxter. Nobody else is to leave this room."

Chapter 42

When Hart was gone, Dani turned to the housekeeper, who was standing silently by an ornate jardiniere in the corner of the room. "When Helen went to get a glass of water from the kitchen earlier, she said you were in the utility room, filling the dishwasher. But when Morag went in a few minutes later, you were gone. Where did you go, Mrs Noble?"

"I went to turn down the beds for the guests. It's what Mrs Raven expects me to do after the meal is finished."

"Did you see Helen when you went to do this?"

She shook her head. "I didn't see anyone. I was too busy smoothing sheets."

"But it doesn't seem possible you didn't see the person who pushed Helen down the stairs when you were actually on that floor at the same time," Oliver said impatiently.

"Well I didn't. Don't you think I would have said if I did?"

"And where's your bedroom located?" Oliver's face was an unpleasant sneer.

"It's across the landing from the rest of you guests, opposite Mr and Mrs Raven."

"Okay, thank you Mrs Noble," Dani added, thinking she would question the woman more closely when they had some privacy.

"Why don't you all have a bloody drink?" Bernie suggested, his voice becoming a little slurred.

"Actually, I don't think that's such a bad idea," James replied, moving over to the cabinet and bringing out a tumbler. "Anyone else?"

It turned out they all needed a drink, except for Mrs Noble, who appeared to be constantly on duty and Dani herself who knew she needed to remain sober and in charge of the situation.

While the others knocked back their whiskies and brandies, Dani went across the hallway to check on Helen.

The woman was asleep. Dani felt her forehead, which was clammy to the touch. At least the painkillers had kicked in, but she was concerned about possible infections if the wound on her leg was left untreated. Although, she also desperately wanted to wait for medical assistance before attempting to re-set the leg.

At first light, someone would be able to follow that path to the town and bring assistance back with them. That thought was giving her hope. She got to her feet and turned towards the grate, tossing another couple of logs onto the dwindling flames.

Jet came to sit by her leg. She stroked the soft fur on his back. "What a mess we're in, eh, boy? If only you could tell us who gave you those nasty tablets?" The dog stared at her with innocent eyes and a puzzled turn of the head. "I suppose they could have gone into your food bowl easily enough." She chuckled. "You've no idea what I'm going on about, have you?"

She headed towards the door, it wouldn't be wise to leave the others on their own for too long. A muffled thud came from the floor above. It must be DC Hart performing his search of the rooms. She left swiftly, pulling the door gently closed behind her.

*

Morag glanced up expectantly when Dani re-entered the library. "How is she?"

"Sleeping, but she feels a little clammy. I hope there's no infection in the wound."

Morag gripped her tumbler of brandy tightly. "I've got the bandage strips and splint ready to bind up her leg, but I'm frightened the shock of moving the bone may be too much for her."

Dani was thinking exactly the same. But they couldn't leave her as she was for much longer, time was running out. If they found the medical bag and that phial of morphine, it might just about be possible to perform the medical procedure here at the house. Her thoughts were interrupted by the sound of footsteps on the stairs. Hart was returning.

All eyes in the library were directed towards the man as he entered the room. The downturned set of his mouth dashed their hopes. "I'm sorry, I couldn't find them. I went through everyone's room thoroughly. Tried to find loose floorboards, searched wardrobes on my hands and knees. Nothing."

The silence was thick with foreboding.

"There's a linen cupboard on that floor too," Morag added hopefully, "there's a space behind the tank where something could be hidden?"

"I looked there too." Hart put his hands in the pockets of his corduroy trousers. "No sign of the items we're looking for."

Dani stepped towards James and took a swig from his tumbler of whisky. "Listen," she said with feeling. "Someone in this room must have taken that medical bag. I don't know why they wanted it, but right now, I don't care. Helen is in that other room in an awful condition, with the sort of pain we've been able to treat since Victorian times. I don't think you expected her to be so badly hurt. All you wanted was that key. If you have any conscience at all, you must let us have that morphine phial back. We can treat her leg break and save her from what could well turn into sepsis by morning. I beg of you to do this." Dani felt her voice cracking, so she gulped down more of the amber spirit, feeling it warm her chest as it slipped down.

Hart stepped forward. "DCI Bevan is right. We don't have a murder on our hands here yet, but if we leave Mrs Baxter in that state for much longer, we will do. Now, this is a highly unorthodox suggestion, but I'm going to make it anyway. I suggest that you all go back to your own rooms. I will sit up with Mrs Baxter in the drawing room and I shall keep the door closed. I want you all to try and get some sleep, but I want the person who took the medical bag to leave some morphine and," he glanced at Dani.

"Any antibiotics in the thermos compartment."

"Leave these items on the hall table before the sun comes up." He raised his hands in the air. "This isn't a trap, I'm not going to leave my phone recording whoever comes down those stairs, I swear to you. We just need those medicines to help Helen."

Dani nodded. "I know it's certainly not in the police handbook, but we aren't operating in normal circumstances here. We all retire to our rooms and stay there. Then, by morning, I pray we'll find the drugs we need to save Helen's life."

The occupants of the library glanced at one another, all of them nodding in agreement. It seemed they had a plan.

Chapter 43

Sunlight was spilling underneath the chintzy curtains when Dermot's eyes opened. For a moment, he had absolutely no idea where he was. He lifted his head off the pillow and glanced down at his body, fully clothed and smothered in a duvet with a cover decorated in flowers and fairies.

He blinked vigorously, then remembered where he was. He must have fallen asleep on Sharon's sofa and she'd got him a duvet and pillow, letting him sleep where he lay, removing only his shoes which had been placed neatly under the coffee table. For one uncharitable moment, he wondered what she'd put in that final mug of tea he'd drunk.

As he levered himself up on an elbow, he begrudgingly accepted he'd had a decent night's sleep, possibly the best he'd had in ages. The flat was quiet. Dermot knew Sharon was on the later shift today and Jackson would no doubt have the impressive lying-in capacity of all teenagers.

He pulled on his shoes and decided to grab a coffee on his way to Pitt Street. The detective slipped out of the flat quietly, fleetingly wondering if he should leave a note and then dismissing the idea as fanciful. Sharon knew exactly where he'd gone. She was the one who'd laminated the damn Christmas week rota.

Dermot took a deep breath as he climbed behind the wheel of his car. It was the day before New Year's Eve. Serena would be home from her parents' house that evening, expecting him to have planned something exciting, romantic and expensive for them to do to see in the New Year. He was still jointly responsible for Jackson and would either have to be babysitting him or on duty at the station on the last day of December so Sharon could look after the lad. He'd already missed Christmas Day. His fiancée would be fuming.

Then there were the Fleetwoods. They had been due to fly home in 24hrs time. This would be the point when Jackson found out his entire family were missing. That they didn't care enough about him to return and face the music, even his own mother. He and Sharon would have to pick up the pieces.

Before Dermot could turn the key in the ignition his phone began to buzz in his top pocket. He reached for it eagerly. "DI Muir."

"Morning, Detective, I hope it's not too early to call. It's Josh Shaw, from West Side BMW."

"Not at all, I'm on my way into the department. Do you have any news for me?"

"Yes, I might have. I called round all my team and emailed those I couldn't reach. One of my colleagues had emailed back late last night, I only just picked it up."

"Oh yes?" Dermot tried not to get excited.

"His name is Neville Thomas, he's worked with us for many years. He doesn't own a holiday home in Tenerife."

Dermot's hopes crashed.

"But his parents do. They bought it two years ago by releasing equity in their house in Newton Mearns. Neville said he was complaining about it to anyone who would listen because the money would all have to be paid back by him and his brother after his folks passed away and the place was barely used, sitting empty for most of the year."

"And you thought Steve Fleetwood might just have remembered this piece of information he'd been told a couple of years back?"

"It occurred to me, yes. I mean, it would be a risk, wouldn't it? Turning up out of the blue to a holiday property. They could well have found it in use."

"But then again, they could well have found it empty. I'm assuming Neville's parents are Mr and Mrs Thomas. If Steve knew the area their holiday home was in, I don't suppose it would have been difficult to ask around a bit and locate it. They must seem pretty harmless; a man on holiday with his wife and two kids. Did Neville give you an address for the place?"

"Yes he did. I will forward it to you now on your work email."

"Thanks Mr Shaw, this may just be the breakthrough we needed."

*

DCS Douglas was leaning over the desk, reading the email on the screen. "The address is in Puerto de la Cruz. How far is that from where the Fleetwoods' hotel was?"

"About a forty minute taxi ride. There are local buses that run the route too. I've already contacted the local Policia. They're sending officers to the address. If they are there and have broken into the place, the Spanish authorities can arrest them, even without the European Arrest Warrant having come through yet, can't they?"

"Yes, they can. Let's hope Mr and Mrs Thomas hadn't left a spare key under a potted palm. It wouldn't be the first time it's happened. Steve could claim they'd been invited to use it."

"Then I will need the Thomas family to confirm he wasn't. I'll get a statement as soon as I hear back from Tenerife."

Douglas took a chair. "Any news from Dani?"

"I'm afraid not. The lines still seem to be down."

"I've spoken to the local station. They were going to try and get a man through. Let's hope he's made contact. What about your research into the guy who owns the place – Raven, is it?"

Dermot sighed. "We found out he hasn't always been called Raven. He changed his name in 2006. That's why we couldn't find out anything about him before that."

"What was he called before?"

"We don't know yet. But I'm working on it."

Douglas sucked his teeth. "I wish we knew more about what Dani was dealing with. Well, whatever you've got so far, send it over to me. I'll carry on where you left off and liaise with Sharon."

Dermot's mouth dropped open. "You're taking me off the case! What have I done wrong?"

"Absolutely nothing. But if the Fleetwoods are arrested by the Spanish Policia today, I'm going to need an officer to go out to Tenerife to bring them back to Glasgow. I'd like that to be you."

Dermot gulped. Deep in his gut he was itching to get out to Spain and get hold of the Fleetwood family. He might even be able to wheedle some information out of them during the flight back. Then he imagined what Serena would say when he told her about this last-minute trip to a tropical island that didn't include her and his mouth went dry. "Of course Sir. As soon as I get news from my police contact, I'll book the earliest flight."

Chapter 44

Despite the adrenaline running through Dani's system each time she heard a bump or a creak on the old wooden floorboards outside in the corridor, she managed to resist the urge to look and did actually drop off for an hour or so.

Beside her, James was anaesthetised with single malt and had been sleeping heavily for most of the night. She was glad, they would need all their energy for what lay ahead.

The sky was finally turning lilac above the bank of trees and Dani decided it was time to pull on her clothes and go out to investigate.

The house was still in semi-darkness. Dani hoped desperately they'd given the person who stole the medical bag enough time to deposit the equipment they needed for Helen on the hall table. It'd been six hours since they all left the library. If this person was going to do it, she decided they'd have done it by now.

She crept down the wide staircase, letting out a gush of withheld breath when she saw several pieces of white plastic lined up along the inlaid mahogany of the table.

Dani jogged the final few paces and examined what was there; an unopened packet of disposable syringes and another of plastic gloves. A glass phial of clear liquid and an opaque plastic bottle, both with printed labels on the side. Her heart hammered in her chest. The irresistible urge was to leave them untouched in order for a forensic team to dust for prints, but this was not the object of the exercise. Normal police procedure was going to have to wait.

Not wanting to leave them out of her sight, Dani bundled up the items in her arms and took them to the drawing room, knocking on the door with her elbow

Within seconds, DC Hart pulled it open. "Oh, thank God!" He declared when he saw what was cradled in Dani's hands.

"The stuff was there when I came down the stairs. We don't have a minute to lose. I'll go and get Morag. You gently wake Helen, we need to get the morphine in her system so we can perform the procedure as soon as possible."

*

They had manoeuvred Helen so her back was resting on cushions. Morag was seated beside her on the stool, in surgical gloves.

"Okay, Helen, you're going to need to talk me through this," Morag said, in as confident a voice as she could muster in the circumstances.

"Yes, I will." She turned her pale face towards DC Hart. "You're sure Allan and my son are okay?"

He nodded. "Yes, I saw them with my own eyes. We just need to get you sorted now."

She managed a weak smile. "And how did you get hold of this equipment, again?"

"No need to worry about that, Helen. Just concentrate on recovering." Dani stood back a little, observing the events.

"You will need to withdraw the correct amount of morphine from the phial using a clean syringe."

Morag did as she was told, her hands remarkably steady. "Okay, I'm taking 10mg as agreed. I can always top you up when we set the leg."

"Yes, about as much as we would use for a small horse. I'd find that funny if the situation weren't so dire."

"It's best you don't make me laugh right now, anyway."

"Check there aren't any air bubbles. Find a fleshy spot at the top of my arm and give it a rub. It doesn't really matter where. Then prick the skin with the needle at 90 degrees and slowly release, hold the skin flat with your other hand if you find it makes it easier."

The room fell absolutely silent, even Jet seemed to be holding his breath.

"Okay, it's in," Morag whispered.

"It won't take long for the morphine to take its effect. If you're going to re-set my leg, now is the time."

The three of them worked swiftly. Duncan Hart held Helen's shoulders firmly. Dani and Morag found the splint and the bandage strips ripped from a clean sheet in one of the bedrooms where the hostess had left it.

Dani looked up to see that Hart was holding both of Helen's hands firmly. He was whispering encouragement in her ear, talking about the wildlife in the glen and the hills and lochs they both must have known so well.

Morag nodded to Dani.

"Okay Helen, we're going to re-set the bone now." She performed the procedure quickly and without hesitation.

Helen let out a low moan.

The women then worked swiftly to attach the splint and bind it firmly into place with the bandages. When they had finished, Morag took one of the spare strips and wiped her friend's brow with it. "You've been so very brave. Now I want you to let the morphine do its job and get some sleep."

Helen's eyes slowly closed.

Dani gathered together the medical equipment. "Is there somewhere secure we can keep these?"

"There's a safe in Bernie's office, but I'll put the bottle of antibiotics in the fridge. As soon as she wakes up, I'll start a course by mouth. Just as a precaution."

"You seem very capable in medical matters?" Dani was genuinely impressed.

"I'm an only child. My mother was ill for a while with cancer. Dad fell apart a little bit and I took over much of the day-to-day care. She's got the all-clear now, otherwise I'd never have gone to live so far away after marrying Bernie."

Dani was surprised by this piece of information. Morag was more down-to-earth than she'd imagined. The lady of the manor act was an affectation, at least in part.

They were about to leave Helen in peace to get some rest when there came an ear-splitting scream. It seemed to echo through the entire house. For a moment, Dani glanced at their patient, thinking the scream was a delayed reaction to the painful procedure they'd just performed on her without anaesthetic, but Helen's face was entirely impassive, she remained fast asleep.

Chapter 45

They ran out into the hall. The scream came again, just as wild and uncontrolled as the first time.

"It's coming from upstairs," Hart said.

"Morag, go and put that medical stuff straight into your husband's safe. This could be another distraction tactic."

She nodded and dashed up the stairs ahead of them.

By the time Dani and DC Hart reached the second floor landing, Oliver and James were standing outside their rooms in their pyjamas. Bernie was in the doorway of his study, as if interrupted at his desk.

"I think it's Dotty!" James called over.

Dani moved swiftly to the door of the Shannahans' room, she knocked loudly. "Tony! Dotty! Is everything okay?"

They heard another cry from within, this time a more muted wail. Dani opened the door without waiting to be summoned.

The scene within the room was bizarre. The curtains were half closed and the morning light lay across the bed in a thick stripe. Dotty was gripping the duvet up to her neck, her face a grimace of terror.

Beside her, lying on his back, was Tony. His eyes were bulging open and a trickle of foamy vomit leaked from his gaping mouth. Dani's vision was immediately drawn to the man's neck, where a plastic syringe was protruding at right angles, the needle still stuck rigid in a vein.

Hart pushed past her and rushed to the bed. He placed a finger under the man's left earlobe, feeling for a pulse. He shook his head at Dani, a grave expression on his face.

Dani moved to Dotty's side of the bed. "Come on now, you're going to need to get up. You've had a terrible shock. There's nothing more we can do here for Tony except leave things exactly as they are."

The older lady gazed at her with wild, confused eyes. "I told him we shouldn't come here! He said we had to, otherwise Bernie would destroy us. Well, he's certainly destroyed us now, hasn't he?"

*

Mrs Noble had made tea for them all. Nobody seemed to have the appetite for breakfast. She'd prepared Dotty's with several heaped spoonfuls of sugar.

Tony's wife was seated at the kitchen table, shaking uncontrollably. Morag was encouraging her to take tiny sips of the sweet liquid. The woman's mouth was clamped shut like a recalcitrant toddler.

The others congregated out in the hall.

"Is he definitely dead?" Oliver asked plaintively. "We didn't even try and resuscitate him."

"There was no question," Hart replied. "His body was stone cold. I reckon he died at least three hours ago."

Dani had seen many dead bodies in her career. She knew Hart's assessment was about right. The thought of Tony's contorted face made her feel sick. They'd decided to send the group up to their beds, a gamble in order to gain the medical supplies for Helen. As a direct consequence of that decision, one of them was dead.

As if he could tell what she was thinking, James took hold of Dani's hand and squeezed it. "We had to do it," he said levelly. "Helen wouldn't have survived without treatment."

"What was injected into him, do you think?" Oliver looked frightened to hear the answer.

"Allan had any number of drugs in that bag which could have caused an overdose. There were tranquilisers and barbiturates, enough to kill a large bull. I should know, I watched him do it once. I expect a *post mortem* will tell us more. A life for a life," Bernie said solemnly. "Both of them my friends. I should never have invited them here."

"Why the hell did you?" Oliver cried. "Sasha couldn't say no to you; her rich, mysterious uncle who'd hardly given her the time of day since she was born! Why did you have to make us come here with those invitations?"

Bernie shook his head, as if he was as confused as Dotty.

Dani stepped forward. "Dotty blames you for her husband's death. Did she watch you administer the contents of that syringe into Tony's neck last night?"

Bernie's face flushed red. "Of course not. I was in bed next to Morag all night."

"But not whilst Morag was helping to treat Helen," Oliver spat.

"That was a good few hours after Tony was already dead," Dani clarified. "But anyone could have slipped out earlier in the night without our bedfellows noticing, I'm sure. A great deal of spirits were drunk in the library before we came up."

"Oliver and Mrs Noble were on their own all night," Bernie put in. "They could have been moving about the house freely enough."

Oliver clenched his fists, as if he might strike his host where he stood.

"Okay, we'll leave the speculation for now. When the rest of my team get here, you will all be questioned closely. Including Mrs Shannahan, who could herself have killed her husband, waiting until morning to raise the alarm." Hart opened the door to the library. "In the meantime, I suggest we return to one room. If and when people need to use the bathroom, I'll accompany them to the door. In the meantime, I'll seal up the Shannahans' bedroom. We must now consider it a crime scene."

Chapter 46

The warmth seeped pleasantly into Dermot's bones as he exited the airport building. It wasn't hot exactly in the north of Tenerife but after the snowy conditions he'd left behind him, the blue skies and sun felt like paradise.

Sargento Nuñez was standing by a squad car on the taxi rank outside, scanning the arrivals spilling onto the concourse for the Scottish detective. Dermot saw his contact first, approaching him with his hand outstretched.

"Glad you could make it here so quickly," Nuñez said with a nod.

"We've got a young lad back in Glasgow who needs to be reunited with his parents," Dermot explained.

The Sargento wasted no time in placing Dermot's suitcase in the boot and opening the passenger door. They sped away from the airport and followed signs to Santa Cruz and the main police station.

The scenery they passed was lush and mountainous. Nuñez pointed out the Cañadas mountain range to the south of them. Dermot hadn't realised how stunning the scenery was on this package holiday island.

"A team arrived at the Thomas property in Puerto de la Cruz late last evening. As you had suggested, we found the family camping out at the house. At first, Señor Fleetwood claimed he was a guest of the Thomas family, but we later discovered a broken pane of glass in the back door leading to the terrace. We also had a copy of the statement the owners had made that no such invitation has been extended."

"Have they been arrested?"

"Sī, the family are at the station in Santa Cruz being questioned. We have charged them with allanamiento de morada. I'm not sure what your equivalent would be?"

"Breaking and entering," Dermot replied. "There's also a crime of squatting back home in Scotland, if a person remains in a property they don't own for any length of time."

Nuñez smiled. "Yes, I know the word, *squat*. Like a lizard on a rock."

"Your English is impeccable."

"This is a holiday island, we have many British tourists and residents here. I learnt the language long ago."

"Have the Fleetwoods been co-operative?"

"The couple are refusing to say a word until they have a British lawyer present. The consular official reached the station a few hours ago but he cannot persuade them to speak. Maybe you will have more luck?"

Dermot stared out of the window at the profusion of marguerite daisies which covered the rocky hillsides, knowing back home in Scotland that sprinkling of white on the hills would be snow, hoping sincerely that he did.

*

After a brief conversation with the official from the small British consulate on the island, Dermot was led to an interview room where Mr and Mrs Fleetwood were seated at a wooden desk, dressed incongruously in shorts and t-shirts.

Dermot had already seen the two younger children, playing table tennis in a recreation room under the watchful eye of a woman officer of the Policia.

The Scottish detective entered the room and took a seat opposite the couple, he introduced himself for the camera recording the entire exchange. "As you have been made aware, you have been arrested under Spanish law for breaking and entering into a property not owned by you. This is a crime taken very seriously on this island, but the authorities are willing to allow you to return to the UK, accompanied by myself, to face charges of child neglect resulting in serious risk of harm to your eldest child, Jackson Fleetwood. Do you understand the charges being made against you?"

"Yes," Steve muttered.

Liz Fleetwood stared at the hands she was wringing in her lap.

"If you come back with me to the UK, you are unlikely to face a custodial sentence. If you stay here, you will be remanded in a Spanish jail and your children sent home without you. You will also not get a chance to see Jackson again for a very long time. Is that what you want?"

Liz whipped her head up. Her eyes were wet with tears. "Have you seen Jackson? Is he okay?"

Dermot had wondered when the couple were ever going to ask. "Yes, he's absolutely fine. We weren't able to find foster accommodation for him, due to the time of year, but he is being looked after by one of our female officers. He has his own room and plenty of home cooked food. I can personally vouch for the high level of his care."

The tears escaped onto her cheeks. "Thank God. We didn't want to leave him, I swear. But he was just being so difficult. He said he was going to stay at his friend's house. But the minute we got on that plane I knew I'd made a terrible mistake."

"You can tell all that to the judge," Dermot said dryly.

Steve leant forward. "Have you got kids?"
Dermot shook his head.

"You love them with all your heart but sometimes they treat you so badly, give you so much trouble over so many months, years even, that you despair of what to do with them. Jackson is jealous of his brother and sister. Whatever we do for them, he sets out to ruin. He was number one with us for so many years, now he's got to share that spot with his siblings, he can't take it. I wasn't having him ruin this trip. We'd been under a lot of pressure recently, we needed to get away."

Dermot felt frustration bubbling up in his chest. "There are organisations that can help if you are suffering from family issues such as those you describe. Jackson was left alone in your house whilst a group of robbers entered the property. He had to hide in a cupboard until they were gone. He was terrified."

Liz started sobbing. "I thought he was at a friend's house," she mumbled into a tissue.

"But did you ring that friend's parents, just to check? Because it wasn't alright with them, they refused. They had no idea Jackson was going to be on his own."

"No, I didn't. I was too ashamed we were going without him."

Dermot knew he needed to stop unleashing his anger on this couple. He needed their co-operation. "Then why didn't you return to Scotland two days ago? Why break into a property you knew was empty but would get you into even further trouble with the authorities? It doesn't make any sense to me."

Steve laid his hand on his wife's arm, as if giving her a command. "No comment. We won't say any more until we have a lawyer back home."

Dermot ran a hand through his hair. "But you will accompany me back to Prestwick?"

Steve nodded. "Yes, we will. But I want my lawyer with us as soon as we land. We won't speak another word until we see him."

Dermot sighed. "If you give me his number, I can have that arranged for you."

Chapter 47

Sharon was determined to show DCS Douglas all the research they had compiled so far into Bernard Raven.

Jackson sat at the workstation with them, but so far Douglas hadn't made any moves to exclude him from the discussions. Sharon supposed they weren't actually investigating a live case, just watching Dani's back.

She laid the notes out in front of the senior officer. "This is a print-out from the Companies House website. From when Raven Homes was first established, their estates were selling houses at a good profit. Raven obviously had a decent team of contractors already in place."

Douglas nodded. "Yes, I agree. Whatever his name was before 2006, I've no doubt he had been involved in the building trade for a long time. Perhaps he was leaving behind bad debts when he decided to change his identity? Have you looked up any individuals who were declared bankrupt in the couple of years before the name change? Particularly from the building trade?"

"No, I haven't," Sharon said. "Good idea. Jackson, can you check that out? What do we need to look at?"

"The insolvency register," Douglas stated. "You can access it through the government website. Look through the entries carefully, Jackson. People who fly close to the wind with their financial practices often try hard to leave no trace. It may be catalogued under a business name, with our Bernie logged as a director or employee somewhere."

"Sure," Jackson replied. "I'll be very thorough." The lad sipped his cup of coffee. "Do you know yet when my parents are due to land?"

"The plane should be landing at around 7pm. DI Muir will be bringing your parents here to the station for questioning. I'm afraid you won't be able to see them until child services decide how they are going to proceed. Sharon will make sure you're back at her flat when they get here."

"What about Emily and Oscar?" Jackson asked the question timidly, as if he didn't have the right to know.

"Like you, they will become wards of the court. We will find them temporary accommodation. But I'm confident that with supervision instated, you will all be re-united in due course."

Jackson's expression brightened. He turned his attention back to his computer screen.

Douglas skimmed through the list of Raven Homes' early developments. "Do we have a map showing where these developments were built? It might give us an idea of where Raven was operating out of. As time goes on, his projects spread further throughout Scotland, but in the first couple of years, they seem centred around the east of Glasgow."

Sharon reached for one of her maps, this one of the city of Glasgow and central Scotland. She began plotting the locations of Raven's early builds with a red marker pen. DCS Douglas was correct, a distinct pattern was emerging.

Douglas ran his finger over the map. "Okay, there's a development in Wishaw and another in Crossford. Then we have the contentious housing estate in Burnt Mills. Most of them are clustered around the M74 in Lanarkshire."

"Yes, they seem to all be close to Motherwell," Sharon continued.

Douglas rubbed his forehead, seemingly deep in thought. "I have a sense this all means something. The Motherwell area and Raven Homes." He repeated the words several times under his breath.

Sharon had never seen Douglas work on an investigation before and she was taken aback at what seemed like his distinctly odd methods.

He slammed his hand down on the desk, making Sharon jump.

"Ravenscraig," he declared loudly.

"Sorry, boss. You've lost me."

"The Ravenscraig Steelworks, operated by British Steel, it was located in Motherwell, North Lanarkshire."

"Ah, yes. They had strikes there in the 80s. I remember it as a child. There were nasty clashes between strikers and police."

"My father was on duty during some of the worst skirmishes," Douglas explained. "The industrial disputes of the 70s and 80s were very difficult years for my family. I recall my father being spat at in the street one time."

"Do you think Bernard Raven has something to do with the steelworks?" Sharon's tone was sceptical.

"He obviously knew the Motherwell area well. All his early projects as director of Raven Homes were located around there. And the choice of 'Raven' as a name; for him and the business. Anyone of his generation who came from the area would be well aware of Ravenscraig, it would be a name etched into their hearts. The town was known for the outline of the three cooling towers of the works, they could be seen from miles away. Hell, Motherwell was even known as 'Steelopolis' until the place finally closed in the early 90s. The whole area is now a new town, totally re-generated. But you can't erase the memory of the steelworks from the hearts of those who worked there."

Sharon dropped into a chair. "Then what does it mean?"

"The plant became a focus of industrial action during the miner's strike of the 1980s. The threat of privatisation brought strikers out in their hundreds. But if Ravenscraig stopped production for even a day, the entire plant would have to be closed. The huge coke ovens needed to be constantly heated or they would cease operation. They had to be kept open and operating for Ravenscraig to survive. But there was a complete breakdown in communication between bosses and unions, the workers seemed not to understand. On the 3rd May 1984 tensions reached a head. Strikers clashed with the police trying to keep the plant open and allow workers who weren't striking to get into the plant. 300 strikers were arrested and the police suffered dozens of injuries amongst its officers. In the end, a procession of trucks managed to get through, but the picketers were pelting them with stones and bottles."

"You seem to know a lot about it."

"My father was on duty that day. He was positioned on one of the road bridges outside the plant. He saw what his colleagues were facing on the frontline. It was terrifying. There were so many injuries."

Sharon glanced at the papers that were scattered on the desk around them. "What do you think Bernard Raven has to do with this steelworkers strike 37 years ago?"

"I'm not sure, but it's something important. Something that made him name himself and his company in some kind of memorial to it."

"Then we'd better find out," Sharon added, with determination in her voice.

Chapter 48

The library had fallen into an uneasy silence. Dotty Shannahan had been given some of Helen's tranquilisers and she dozed in the chair by the fire.

Oliver stood a few feet from her, gripping the edge of the mantelpiece, his knuckles pure white.

Bernie was pacing up and down by the bay window. Gazing out every few steps at the snow still lying thickly outside and the fat flakes falling from the sky creating a brand new layer. "We need to follow the track Allan and the others made to Inverlael before it's covered again by fresh snow. A proper police presence is needed here. We've got a *dead body* upstairs for pity's sake."

"That journey will be made, I can assure you," DC Hart added smoothly. "But I need to know that when I leave, the rest of you will be safe until we return."

"Because there's a crazed murderer amongst us, you mean?" Oliver hissed. "I for one would rather face the elements than stay here to be butchered."

Dani raised her hand in a placatory gesture. "I suggest that Mrs Noble prepares us a trolley of tea and cakes. I can accompany her to the kitchen whilst she prepares it."

"No thanks," Oliver sneered. "I don't enjoy arsenic in my morning coffee."

"There's no arsenic in that medical bag," Bernie said impatiently. "It's not something animals require for treatment."

"Well, ground up ketamine or something," he retorted.

"Actually, it would have contained pentobarbital, Helen told me earlier, when she'd woken up and I told her the terrible news." Morag ventured.

"What does that do?" James looked expectantly at their host.

"It's used to euthanise animals. But would have the exact same effect on humans. She thinks it is what was probably injected into Tony."

James gulped. "I've suddenly lost my appetite."

Oliver took a step into the centre of the room. "What the hell are we waiting for?"

"I suspect DC Hart is waiting for a break in the weather sufficient for his colleagues to get here by road. Helen is stable now and there's nothing more that can be done for Tony. I don't think he's got any intention of leaving us all here alone," James added.

Hart remained silent, as if confirming the point.

Oliver stormed out into the hall. "Well sod that idea. I'm not waiting until nightfall where we can be picked off again like fish in a barrel."

Bernie followed him out. "What are you doing, Oliver? Don't be a fool. You're safer here with the police. We've got plenty of food and water left."

Oliver gave a humourless laugh. "You've got to be kidding. The woman serving us our food may already have poisoned one of us!" He made a move towards the boot room, where they had left the outdoor gear two nights before.

Dani and James ran after him. "Listen, Oliver. I know we can't keep you here, but you shouldn't go alone. You don't have any knowledge of the area. I suspect you don't even know what direction Inverlael is in. Do you?"

Oliver paused during the process of pulling on his padded jacket. "No, I don't."

"Then wait five minutes and we'll get a party together," Dani reasoned. "I'm as keen to go for help as you are."

*

They stood in a circle in the middle of the library, like conspirators plotting revolution.

DC Hart was the first to speak. "Dotty and Helen are too frail to leave the house. I also suggest Mrs Noble stays here, as she can prepare the food for those who remain."

"I will have to stay to look after Helen," Morag stated, tears smudging her almond eyes.

"And I'm going nowhere without my wife," Bernie added firmly.

"Then we have our group," DC Hart announced. "I shall stay here with those remaining at the house. I will keep everyone in the library as far as is possible. We will wait for assistance to arrive."

Dani nodded, the division of people seemed a sensible one. "Then James, Oliver and I will head for Inverlael to raise the alarm."

"Then you should hurry," Bernie said. "You'll need all the daylight there is left. And bloody good luck to you."

Chapter 49

Jackson glanced up eagerly from the screen of his computer. "I think I've got something!"

Sharon and DCS Douglas moved round the desk to stand behind him.

The lad pointed at the lines of data on the government website. "According to the Insolvency Register, a company in Wishaw went into liquidation in January 2005. The name was Motherwell Building Contractors Ltd and the director was listed as Bernard Ernest Corder."

Douglas squinted at the screen. "The date seems about right and the area certainly tallies with where Raven was operating his business after 2006."

"Bernard Corder," Sharon repeated under her breath. "Could this be the man now calling himself Raven?"

Douglas shrugged his broad shoulders. "I suggest we dig into this Bernard Corder's past a little further and we may well find out." He patted Jackson on the back. "Well done, my lad. Very well done."

*

The snow was still falling in light flakes, the wind was whipping the tiny crystallised hexagons into the faces of the group trudging along the edge of the frozen loch.

Oliver was striding off ahead. Dani hoped that in his eagerness he didn't fall and break his ankle. Then they would be in real difficulties.

Dani and James kept pace side-by-side. They could identify the path the others had already cleared two days before but it was now covered in sheets of ice, with a fresh swathe of snow over the top making every step treacherous.

With Oliver out of earshot, James turned to Dani. "There's something I need to tell you."

Dani felt her body turn even colder. A band of dread tightened once again around her chest. "What is it?"

"Do you remember I called you on Christmas Eve to tell you we'd been invited up here?"

"Of course." It was only a few days before, but it now felt like a lifetime.

"I didn't quite tell you everything."

Dani trudged on in silence, waiting for him to continue.

"Bernie had called to invite me to his place for the festive season. I wanted to keep him as a client, gain more business if I could, so I accepted the invite. But I told him I would come alone. I didn't think I could possibly ask you to travel to such a Godforsaken place as this and stay for so long. But when I said I wasn't going to bring you, Bernie became very insistent. He didn't seem interested in me coming at all without you tagging along." He took a deep breath of freezing air, setting his teeth on edge. "So I set out to persuade you. I was so desperate for Bernie's favour that I made you come here, exposed you to a bloody murderer for heaven's sake."

Dani gripped his arm. "It was my decision to come. Nobody makes me do anything I don't want to do." Despite her words, she still felt a stab of hurt. She didn't know why James hadn't told her sooner. "But what does it mean? That Bernie wanted me here so badly? Did he know I was a senior police officer?"

"I don't know. I didn't think so at the time, I only referred to you as my partner, Dani. But I suppose it was naïve to imagine a man like that wouldn't know everything about us."

Dani didn't reply, but she felt it was very naïve, and potentially dangerous.

They continued their trek in silence. Dani looked out across the glen as the snow began to clear. She was keeping Oliver in her line of sight up ahead. Fortunately, he was wearing the same lurid ski jacket he'd been sporting all week.

Dani was lost in her thoughts. If Bernie had been planning murder this week, why would he be so keen to have a high-ranking police officer present? Or perhaps he sensed he was in danger himself of some kind. She couldn't get out of her mind what Sasha had said about this week being a kind of celebration. But what role could she possibly play in that?

The questions constantly nagging at the edge of Dani's consciousness were supressed when she saw Oliver stop dead in his tracks up ahead. She turned to James and crinkled her brow.

"What's the matter?" James called over, his tone wary.

They picked up their pace, carefully negotiating the ice and snow until they reached the place where Oliver was standing. The man maintained his silence, but he pointed with a shaky hand to a spot about ten feet up the hillside.

Dani crept forward. She could see an odd formation in the snow, like the angels they used to make in the playground at school by lying in the soft white flakes and moving their arms and legs up and down.

This was no snow angel. She saw the black of a thick walking jacket, stark against the white snow. A pair of legs sticking out beneath, lying in a bizarre star shape.

James was beside her, his breathing heavy. "Oh, holy shit."

They were close enough now to see the head. It was turned to one side so that the blank, green eyes seemed to stare right through them. A circle of red bloomed out from the torso and the blade of some kind of weapon protruded from the chest.

"It's Pete Tredegar," Dani whispered, her words taken by the wind and scattered up the glen.

"His body looks frozen solid." James put a gloved hand to his mouth. "I'd say he's been out here for quite some time."

Chapter 50

When Dani and the others had left, DC Hart closed the front door firmly behind them and turned the deadlock, dropping the key into his jacket pocket.

He checked on Helen Baxter, who was sleeping peacefully in the drawing room, no sign of fever or infection. He was glad. It had never been his intention to harm her. She had been an innocent bystander, caught in the cross-fire.

Duncan Hart took a deep breath and approached the library, entering slowly and surveying the scene. Mrs Noble was pouring tea from a trolley. Bernie was still pacing by the window, looking as if he would have liked something stronger than caffeine.

Dotty was still out for the count in the armchair and Morag was sitting stiffly by a shelf of books, her hands clasped in her lap, her fingers nervously twisting her wedding band.

The policeman's face broke into a lazy smile. "Ah, Mr and Mrs Raven, we are alone at long last. I thought we'd never get any privacy."

Morag whipped her head up, an expression of horror forming on her face. "What do you mean?"

Bernie stopped pacing and faced the policeman. "What are you talking about? Who are you?"

Mrs Noble put down the teapot and went to stand beside Hart.

"What the blazes is going on? *Mrs Noble*, what are you doing?"

"She's with him," Morag said shakily.

Bernie took a threatening step forwards, clenching his fists by his sides. "I could take you on, no trouble young man. Just try me!"

"Oh, I know you could," Hart replied evenly. "You're a violent hooligan at heart. But you only like to attack when you're in a gang, don't you? One of a mass of ferocious faces, not brave enough to act on your own."

"Oh, you'll see what I'm capable of. Did you kill Tony?" Bernie's face was puce.

"Poor old 'Taff' Shannahan. He wasn't a violent man, was he? Just incredibly weak and self-serving, but sometimes they can be the worst."

"What is he talking about?" Morag looked at her husband imploringly.

Then Mrs Noble moved as quick as a flash. She was suddenly behind Morag's chair, a full hypodermic needle pressed to a pulsing vein in her boss's neck. She fixed her gaze on Bernie, her eyes full of hate. "Make a move and I'll send this stuff straight into her bloodstream."

Bernie froze to the spot. "What is it?"

"Like Mrs Baxter said, it's a lethal dose of pentobarbital. It's used to put dogs to sleep, except in those cases, it's also mixed with a good dash of tranquiliser, to relax the reflex muscles. It's a nasty death otherwise; convulsions and pain, the expulsion of the body's waste products. Unpleasant really."

Bernie's face contorted into a snarl. "What do you want. Money?"

Hart pursed his lips. "Is that what you think it's all about? I've followed your career over the years; from the thug steelworker Bernard Corder to the fancy industrialist Bernie Raven. But you've never quite shed your criminal side, have you? Oh, Raven Homes is squeaky clean enough, you learnt that lesson after your first company went bust. But you still decided to do your criminal activities on the side. I think it's just in your nature to intimidate and extort from good people."

"What does he mean?" Morag rasped, finding her housekeeper's grip surprisingly strong. "Is this true?"

"Poor Morag," Hart continued. "She doesn't really know anything about this. Not like Elise, your first wife. She found out about your criminal activities and divorced you like a shot, making sure your children wanted nothing more to do with you. I did wonder if that would be punishment enough for me to be satisfied. But it wasn't, I'm afraid. Especially when Mum and I found out about the *pardon*."

Mrs Noble seemed to flinch at the sound of the word.

Morag's expression was confused.

"Oh, that's what we're really here to celebrate, didn't you know, Morag? It's the reason there are a dozen bottles of the finest champagne in your fridge. It's not your fifth wedding anniversary, the passing of another successful year or anything mundane like that."

"Bernie?" Morag turned to her husband questioningly.

His face was like one of the stone statues in their ornamental garden.

"In October of this year," Hart declared, as if addressing a large assembly. "the Scottish Government, in its great wisdom, decided to pardon all those miners and steelworkers involved in the 1984 strikes who had been arrested and convicted of offences during the many clashes between picketers and police. This pardon included expunging the colourful record of a Mr Bernard Corder, who had been convicted of several counts of assault and GBH against police officers during the picketing of the Ravenscraig Steelworks on 3rd May 1984."

"It was a long time ago. I was a young man protecting his livelihood. I got caught up in the violence. I wasn't to blame, we were having our way of life destroyed, our families cast into poverty."

"You know, I actually thought you might confess to what you did that day. What with your wife threatened with an imminent, grisly death. I over-estimated you."

"Is that what you want, a confession? Because I'll give you one." Bernie raised his hands up in supplication.

"Will you? Do you actually realise what you did?"

"I imagine you knew one of the officers gathered that day to hold back the picketers. Many of them suffered terrible injuries, for that I am sorry."

Hart let out a grunt. "Do you realise you were very familiar to the local police back then? You were a rabble-rouser known to enjoy a bit of burglary on the side of your job at the works. A right nasty piece of work. It also meant your face was easily recognisable even in those dense crowds who'd gathered that day." The policeman glanced at Mrs Noble, as if requesting her permission to continue. She nodded solemnly. "Do you remember one particular coach that reached the gates of Ravenscraig that morning? I'd be surprised if you don't, because it was one that contained your *friend* Tony 'Taff' Shannahan. Except he wasn't your friend really. You knew him as a *scab*, a man who'd repeatedly broken the strike to feed his young family." Hart sneered. "Oh, you employed him later, after the works had closed and you'd built a new career for yourself, but only because you felt you could use him. His sons never knew he'd been a scab, had grown up in awe of the strikers. It would have destroyed their respect for him to have found out, so you held that information over Taff for decades. Getting him to work for you and do your dirty deeds under the threat of revealing his grubby secret."

"Is this true?" Morag's features had lost their rigidity. She seemed suddenly a decade older. "Were you blackmailing him? I knew you'd been pardoned by the Crown, but I thought it was just for a breach of the peace. Have you been lying to me?"

Bernie's face remained impassive, his eyes looking only at Duncan Hart. "Tell me about the coach, I think I'm starting to remember."

"The picket lines were surging forward, it was getting difficult for the police cordon to hold off the baying mob. Finally, a few strikers broke through. They surrounded the coach and pelted it with missiles. The windows were covered in mesh so didn't break. Then the mob tried shaking the coach from side-to-side. Apparently, at one point it looked as if the thing might topple completely. One bastard hurled a Molotov cocktail, it missed the vehicle by inches. But for one young policeman present, this was the final straw."

Bernie nodded, as if recalling the scene.

"PC Colin Hart, 29 years old and with a wife and young child at home. He knew his job was to make sure that coach got through, with the workers on board safe. So he stepped into the midst of the crowd. Shouting to distract attention from the bus. It worked. He became a focus for all the hatred and resentment against the police that had bubbled up that day. The crowd around him jostled and punched, shoving him closer and closer to the gates."

Morag closed her eyes tight shut.

"Meanwhile, the coach driver had seen the crowd in front of him thin out, so he took his chance, terrified the vehicle was going to be torched with them all trapped inside if he hung about any longer. The driver jumped on the accelerator. Just as the angry mob were pushing Colin Hart towards the entrance. I'm told there was a scream as the young policeman disappeared under the wheels of the coach, maybe from a woman or youngster in the crowd, perhaps from a fellow officer."

"But he wasn't dead," Bernie breathed. "I remember them carrying him off the road, putting him on a stretcher."

Hart fixed Bernie with a look of disgust. "No, my father wasn't dead. There was still a faint pulse. In fact, he languished in hospital, his bones and body crushed to a near pulp for the next month before he finally gave up the fight. That's why his death was never directly linked to that day of violence at the steelworks. But my mother and I knew exactly who was to blame, and in all these years we never forgot it."

Chapter 51

The wind had picked up, buffeting the trio as they stood in a line on the hillside, absorbing the gruesome scene laid out before them.

"But DC Hart said Pete had stayed in Inverlael with the Baxters' boy. He'd twisted his ankle and couldn't walk?"

James turned to his companion, locking eyes. "He lied."

"Oh shit." Oliver became agitated, scanning the snowy landscape around him. "Then was what he said about Sasha true? Did she really make it to Inverlael to meet up with Dr Huntley? What if he hurt her too?!"

Dani placed a gloved hand on his shoulder. "We have to assume they did reach the town. For Hart to have known all about Allan, Sasha and Tredegar he must have spoken to the group when they arrived at Inverlael. I think Pete never injured himself on the trek. I think they both headed back towards Strathain House that evening, but only one of them made it."

"Hart killed him?" Oliver gaped in disbelief. "But why?"

Dani shook her head gravely. "I've no idea. His warrant card looked genuine."

James was shivering with the cold. "We have to go back to the house. We've left them all in terrible danger."

Dani glanced at her watch. They'd been walking for two and a half hours already. "We're more than halfway there. I say we carry on. Whatever is going on back at that house will need reinforcements to deal with. We aren't going to be much use on our own."

"What about poor Helen and the others?" James's teeth were chattering with both the shock of their discovery and the bitter cold.

"We have to hope they've all stuck together and are safe for the time being. It isn't an easy decision, but we need back-up. If we return now, nobody will know what danger they are all in."

James nodded. "Okay, I agree."

"Me too," Oliver said. "I just want to find out what's happened to Sasha. I mean, I care about the others of course, but my main duty is to my wife, you know?"

Dani understood. In this type of situation, your priorities were usually put into sharp focus. "Then let's head off, and this time we'll keep up with Oliver's pace."

*

DCS Douglas drummed his fingers impatiently on the moulded plastic lid as the papers were slowly dumped out of the department printer. He swiftly scooped them up and deposited them on Sharon's desk.

She picked up the first sheet. "Bernard Ernest Corder was convicted of two counts of grievous bodily harm and one count of common assault at the Sheriff Court in Motherwell on 12th May, 1984. He served three months of a six month sentence at Barlinnie."

"He had been a steelworker at Ravenscraig for five years when the industrial action started," Douglas continued. "But he had several minor convictions for petty theft and breaking and entering going back into his teens."

"He certainly seemed to be right in the thick of the clashes at Ravenscraig on 3rd May 1984." Sharon sighed.

"If my father was still alive I would ask him," Douglas lamented. "He and many of the officers on duty that day remember what happened like the footage was permanently recorded in their heads."

"I'm very sorry he isn't still with us." Sharon's words were genuine. She'd sent Jackson out to get sandwiches from the café next door, unsure of what they may be about to unearth.

"I think I may know why this Christmas has been so special for Bernard."

Sharon eyed him expectantly.

"I don't know if you saw the news coverage a few months ago? But back in October, the First Minister decided to issue a pardon to all those strikers who had received convictions during the industrial action at Scottish steelworks and coal mines in 1984 and '85."

Sharon whistled through her teeth. "So Bernard has had his record wiped clean."

"Yes, and all the others who were arrested that day at Ravenscraig, and across Scotland. To be honest, I'm glad my father isn't here to witness it."

Sharon could imagine how raw the memories were for the police officers involved, even more than 35 years on. She knew the mines and steelworks were a way of life for many men, one they saw as in desperate peril, but so was policing. "After coming out of prison, Bernie appears to have kept his nose clean. It seems he returned to work at the steel plant after leaving prison and remained there until it closed in the early 90s."

"After that, he set up Motherwell Building Contractors. According to Companies House records, it seems to have made reasonable money for a few years. Then the company fell deeper and deeper into debt, finally filing for bankruptcy in 2003. By this time, Bernie had a son and a daughter in their early teens. But his wife, Elise, filed for divorce in April 2003. I couldn't trace their current whereabouts. They must have taken on a new surname, but certainly not their father's." Douglas sighed.

"Sounds like they didn't want anything more to do with Bernie."

"Doesn't it just. His first marriage didn't survive the collapse of his business."

"But a couple of years later, up rises Bernie Raven, top businessman, from the ashes."

Douglas raised an eyebrow at her poetic language, but dipped his head to agree. "A new name and a new business. Now his record has been cleared, his reputation fully restored. He was finally free from the legacy of Ravenscraig. So why the grand house party this week in the Highlands? Perhaps Bernie's dark past wasn't so easy for him to shake off after all?"

Chapter 52

Morag tried to shift her vision to the side, attempting to catch the housekeeper's eye. "Mrs Noble, *Maureen*. We've known one another for three years. Please put down the syringe and let us talk this through without threats. I want to hear your side of things."

Hart laughed, as if genuinely amused. "That's not really her name. My mother is called Alice Hart. She lost her husband after he was crushed under the wheels of a three tonne coach with armoured windows. He didn't look much like the man she married as she sat by his bedside, watching the life drain out of him. Then she had to go home and explain to her four year old why his daddy wasn't ever coming back."

A tear slid down Morag's cheek. "I'm so sorry. I want to find out the truth too. I didn't know any of this."

Hart shook his head. "I don't believe you did. Which is a real shame. You, Mrs Shannahan and Mrs Baxter are unfortunate witnesses to the main event."

Bernie puffed up his chest. "It's me you want, Hart. Let my wife and the other women go."

"Well, I wasn't expecting *that*," Hart said with mock surprise. "I didn't think you were the gallant type, not with what you've been up to in the past few years."

Morag's eyes flickered to her husband.

"That's right. Mum and I moved to Inverlael a few years after dad died. She wanted to get as far away from the memories as possible. We had a small pension from the police, and mum supplemented it with cleaning jobs for local hotels. As soon as I turned eighteen and had my Highers, I went to train at Tulliallan. I wanted to be a policeman like my father. We lived very peacefully for many years. Then, one day, I picked up the local paper and saw that Bernie "Raven" was buying the old ruin of Strathain House. I couldn't believe what I was seeing. The man who pushed my brave father under a truck was staring out at me from the page. About to be our neighbour. I knew your face, of course. One of Dad's colleagues sent mum your mugshot after you were arrested. He said you were the one who gave the final shove, with a gleeful smile on your face."

"It wasn't like that." Bernie had dropped his head.

"SHUT UP! Here you were, flaunting your wealth, even paying tribute to Ravenscraig in your new name, your business. You had no shame."

"What my husband did was awful. Let's get it out in the open, have a proper trial. But not this," Morag whispered between sobs.

Hart ignored her pleas. "Once you'd got the place habitable, you advertised for a housekeeper. That's when we saw our chance. It was easy enough to mock up some references, they were genuine enough, it was just the name we changed. So mum watched you for these last few years, listened to your phone conversations and read your correspondence. You're still being a very naughty boy, aren't you Bernie?"

The man's entire body seemed to sag.

"Why don't you tell us all what you've been up to?"

He shook his head. "You're going to kill us anyway. Why not get it over and done with?"

Hart's mother pushed the needle further into Morag's neck, the woman yelped with fear.

"Okay, your wife first."

"No!" Bernie yelled. "Okay, tell me what you want. I'll do anything you want."

"Good," Hart said calmly. "For a start, get down on your knees."

*

The light was fading when Dani, James and Oliver reached the outskirts of Inverlael. James was holding out his iPhone, searching for a signal, his hand almost too cold to get a grip on the rubbery casing.

"Don't waste time on calling. We'll head straight for the police station," Dani said.

The residents of the pretty Highland town had obviously been out clearing the snow over the previous days. The sight of people walking the streets and the glittering displays of Christmas lights adorning the shop windows raised her spirits.

Dani spotted the illuminated blue sign indicating they'd finally reached their destination. Oliver pushed through the double-doors and Dani pressed her warrant card up to the window of the reception desk.

"We need to speak with your highest ranking officer, and we need it to happen right now."

Chapter 53

Bernie knelt on the Persian rug in the centre of the room, facing the bay window and let his head hang forwards limply. Morag's body had begun to shake, she couldn't control it, although constantly aware of the needle being held precariously close to her throat.

Hart went over to one of the bookcases and pulled something out of a shadowy gap between the shelves.

Morag gasped.

The detective was holding one of the axes they'd been using at the target range on their first day. Hart turned it over in his hand, like it was a piece of sculpture. "I found it under poor Tony's pillow. I think he might have been a bit scared of you Bernie, do you agree?"

Bernie slumped down further towards the floor.

Hart stood behind him and raised the axe above his head. The dying rays of the winter sun glinted on its shiny steel blade.

Morag whimpered. "He doesn't deserve to die."

"Oh, you think so, do you? Well, we'll let you be the judge of that." He reached out with his foot and gave Bernie's leg a nudge. "How about you tell your lovely wife what you've been up to as a little side line for the past few years to supplement your income from the building trade. If you 'fess up, I might spare your missus from such an awful death."

Bernie exhaled a gush of air, as if his entire body was deflating. "I'll tell you it all, if you will spare Morag."

"Go ahead," Hart entreated. "We're in the library, why don't you spin us a good yarn to keep us entertained?"

"What I'm going to say is the absolute truth. There's no point in denying anything now." He wheezed uncomfortably as if the words were stuck in his wind pipe. "About three years ago, I sold a luxury house to a wealthy diplomat in an exclusive gated estate near Kelvin Hall. I saw he had a wife and two young kids moving in there with him. This property was worth several millions, but after build costs, tax and wages, bungs to the councillors, I barely came away with anything. I decided I wanted to live like that. I worked hard enough, why shouldn't I? I'd always dreamt of having a Highland Castle, but I wanted it modern, all-mod cons. With beautiful grounds surrounding it. But there's no way that kind of money can come to you legally."

"So you slipped back into your shady old ways." Hart swung the axe rhythmically above the man's head, like a clock pendulum.

"I knew the floorplans of those executive houses in detail, because my architects had designed them. I knew where the master suite was, and where the children would sleep. My management company even supplied the alarm systems."

"You burgled them?" Morag asked meekly.

Hart scoffed. "Oh, no. There wasn't enough money in that. His plan was far more lucrative, and thoroughly wicked, wasn't it Bernie?"

"Kidnap," the man said hoarsely. "I put together a team who I'd met when I was in Barlinnie or had crossed my path afterwards, who I knew were bent. I knew a guy who worked as a mechanic for a luxury car rental service in the city. He'd fenced some stolen goods for me in the past and was only too keen to earn some serious money. He placed listening devices into the cars of men I'd sold these palatial houses to. Then I knew where they went and when they'd be away on business trips."

"Leaving their wives and children at home."

"I don't believe what I'm hearing," Morag spluttered.

Bernie carried on, but his voice was distant and detached. "Our very first job was the diplomat in Kelvinside. When we knew he was being driven to the airport for a conference, a couple of my men let themselves into the property. They were quick and efficient, gagging and tying up the wife first, then the two kids. We needed to take some videos, make it look nasty. We usually had the money in an overseas account before the morning."

"Don't these people have bodyguards, security protection?" Morag's voice was a croak.

"Yes, but they often remained with the dignitary. We had set up a state of the art security system in these houses, charging them five figure sums for the privilege. It made them feel safe. They had no idea we had the power just to turn it off."

"How often did you do it? Kidnap or threaten to kidnap these mothers and their children?" Morag's voice had become stronger.

"He's been doing it for over three years, Morag. How many do you reckon?" Hart was growing impatient.

Morag gagged. "I think I might be sick."

"Well, I'd look away for this next bit then." Hart raised the axe high in the air above Bernie's neck, the action sent a breeze across the room.

Morag squeezed her eyes shut, but Alice Hart watched as if mesmerised by the movement of the blade, cutting through the heavy atmosphere, racing towards the prone form of her adversary.

Then time seemed to stand still. The blade stopped falling and veered off course, landing with a clatter by the fireplace.

Morag flicked her eyes open. Duncan Hart was tottering on his feet, finally falling like a felled tree onto the carpet next to Bernie. The woman holding her released her grip, running to her son's side. Morag took her chance and leapt up.

That's when she saw a tall figure in a dressing gown by the door to the library, the metal poker from the drawing room fire lying limply in her hand. It was Helen. She was leaning on the frame, her bound leg having been dragged along behind her, the woman's energy now seemingly completely spent.

Morag turned back to view the room, noticing now, the bloody dent in the back of Duncan Hart's skull. His mother was draped over him, sobbing her heart out and her own husband had crawled into a ball on the rug, rocking back and forth on his heels.

Chapter 54

When the officers from Inverlael had beaten down the front door of Strathain House, they were greeted by a baffling scene.

A woman who looked to have been dragged out of a hospital bed was lying across a chesterfield sofa in the hallway, a bloodied fire poker on the floor beside her.

There seemed to be a commotion in what looked like the library. An elderly woman was in a deep sleep in an armchair by a fire now reduced to ashes in the grate. A middle-aged man and woman stood side-by-side but not touching, appearing to be in a state of total shock, a black Labrador sitting obediently by the gentleman's feet.

On the floor lay the body of another man, who he assumed was DC Hart, with what looked like the housekeeper, lying over him, her hand softly caressing his hair. The Detective Inspector almost wanted to look away, rather than be a voyeur to this unsettling display.

The other lady stepped forward. "I'm Morag Raven. This is my husband. We own Strathain House. Is DCI Dani Bevan here with you?"

The detective moved aside. "She's out the front. We wanted to enter the property first, on account of the seriousness of the reports we had received of incidents that had taken place here over the past few days. We had to wait until a utility vehicle with a snow plough arrived from Ullapool to assist us in getting along the road. It held us back by a couple of hours, I'm afraid."

"We're going to need an ambulance. This man has a head injury and our friend has a nasty break to her leg."

The DI nodded. "The ambulance is on its way, it will follow in the tracks we cleared. Now, someone is going to have to explain exactly what has gone on here. Will that be you, madam?"

Morag nodded. "Yes, I will explain everything. Right from the very start. But I will only do that with DCI Bevan present. Without her, I'm not uttering a single word."

Chapter 55

A cardboard tray containing several takeout coffee cups had been placed on top of the haphazard piles of paper printouts on Sharon's workstation.

Dani reached to take one of the cups. "I see you've been keeping the place tidy in my absence."

DCS Douglas gave a sheepish grin. "Sorry, Dani, that's actually my fault. The neatest detective at this desk was young Jackson."

"Yes, I hear I have a new young recruit to my team," she added with a raise of an eyebrow.

"Jackson was really fab," Sharon declared proudly. "He did most of the research on Bernard's financial background. He's studying business studies, you see."

"Where is he now?" Dani asked, her eyebrows crinkled in concern.

Dermot blew on his espresso before volunteering, "He's in the family room with his mum, brother and sister. They're having a session with the officer from Child Protection. I'm hoping there will be a chance of reconciliation."

"What about Steve Fleetwood?" Sharon asked. Since Dermot's return from Tenerife they'd barely had a chance to speak.

"With Morag Raven's testimony about the confessions her husband made the other night, we were able to get a warrant to search Bernard's computer and phone records. It showed communications between Fleetwood and Raven going back four years. He's been charged with conspiracy to kidnap and extortion with menaces. There are multiple offences. All the cars he's worked on have been seized for a full forensic search. With the evidence we have, he's going to prison for a long time. As is Raven himself, although he isn't denying any of the charges. It seems the experience of nearly being beheaded has made incarceration at Her Majesty's pleasure seem not so bad."

"I think Morag told him to confess," Dani continued. "She was utterly disgusted with what she found he'd been up to. I expect she'll give evidence against Bernie if she has to."

Dermot knitted his brow. "We'd been after that kidnapping gang for years. They were operating whilst I was still in the diplomatic service. I saw first hand the pain and trauma their actions caused, to little children too. But they never left a trace, always knowing when to strike and how to disable the alarm systems. Now we know they had insider knowledge. It was a very sophisticated operation."

"So why was Steve so reluctant to return to the UK?" Sharon asked. "Did he think we might have found out about his connection to the kidnappings?"

Dermot sipped his coffee. "Actually, I believe it was because he was scared of Bernie Raven. It was being told of the break-in at his property that frightened Steve, not the thought of being prosecuted for child neglect." He perched on the edge of the desk. "From what I've seen of the exchanges on Bernie's computer, Steve had been falling out of favour. He'd been demanding more and more of a cut of the ransom money they were extracting from their wealthy victims. Bernie had already given Steve one of their newbuilds on the Clyde Wharf for a hugely discount price, but then he starts haggling over the quality of the fittings thrown in, even getting a solicitor involved to put pressure on Raven Homes. I reckon Bernie decided to teach his lackey a lesson."

Sharon widened her eyes. "You think Bernie's men were responsible for the burglary at the Fleetwoods' house?"

"Yes, but I don't believe it was a burglary."

Sharon looked puzzled.

"It has all the hallmarks of one of Bernie's jobs: the intruders knew the layout of the property and that Steve was on holiday. But what I also think they knew, as the management company had full access to all the CCTV to the development, was that Jackson was there on his own."

DCS Douglas sighed heavily. "It was an attempted kidnapping."

Sharon gasped. "You mean that if Jackson hadn't hidden in that cupboard, they would have taken him?" Her heart pounded at the thought, even though the danger had now passed.

Dermot nodded. "They would probably have tied him up and sent footage to Steve, warning him to stop getting greedy. Thankfully, Jackson kept absolutely quiet in his hiding place. The kidnappers must have got spooked for some reason and took off without finding him."

"Jackson told me his mum had that wardrobe system fitted after they moved in, she'd seen an advert on the TV and wanted it. The cost had caused a row between his parents."

Dermot grimaced. "Then it was a part of the interior layout that wasn't on the original plans for the property. That impulse buy saved Jackson from a nasty fate."

Sharon glanced over her shoulder, in the direction of the family room. "Does Jackson have to know about this?"

"I don't think he has to find out he was targeted to be kidnapped, it's pure theory on my part until we get more evidence. But he's going to know all about his father's crimes. The details will all come out in court and we know how adept Jackson is at finding information on the internet."

Sharon's mouth turned down at the corners with sadness. "How much did Liz know about what Steve was doing?"

"She didn't say much in interview, their lawyer saw to that. But Liz claims she had no idea of the nature of Steve's criminal activities. She knew they were getting money over and above his wages at the garage, but she never asked too much about its origins. Her husband told her he was doing chauffeuring work on the side for extra cash."

"But that house they bought was worth hundreds of thousands more than they could ever have afforded on his mechanic's wage. Even with a bit of moonlighting as a driver, She can't possibly have believed the money would have covered it."

"Sometimes, we believe what we want to believe," Dani added quietly.

"Well, I hope the social workers give her the benefit of the doubt," Dermot continued, "because then Jackson, Emily and Oscar will keep one of their parents and will stay out of foster care. Liz claims Steve put her under pressure to go on that holiday without their son. He wanted to get away from his criminal life, if only temporarily. Bernie was already turning the heat up on him. He wasn't going to let a teenager's stubbornness stop him."

"It sounds like Liz Fleetwood is a woman easily led to do the wrong thing, but she's still the children's mother and they're probably better off with her than in the system," Dani said wistfully.

Sharon felt a lump forming in her throat. She gulped down her cappuccino to try and get rid of it, but her eyes were prickling with tears. The thought of never seeing Jackson again was almost more than she could bear.

Dermot seemed to sense her mounting distress. "If Jackson returns to the care of his mother, I'm sure we will still be able to visit him. I don't think Sharon's going to let him rest easy until he has enrolled himself at police college." He winked at his colleague.

She managed a smile, but still couldn't trust herself to speak.

Dani laid a hand on Sharon's shoulder. "I have much to thank you all for. This case with Jackson Fleetwood was a difficult one. The fact you took him in over the Christmas period is to be commended. Not to mention the information you gathered on Raven. With the information we now have on him, that man should be going to prison for a very long time."

Chapter 56

They had just finished their coffees when James stepped out of the lift onto the serious crime floor. He strode over to join the officers.

"Is one of those coffees for me?" He asked brightly.

"Yes, but I expect it's cold by now," Dani replied dryly.

"Apologies, but I just got off the phone from Raigmore Hospital in Inverness."

"How is Helen?" Dani's expression was eager for news.

"The surgery on her leg went well. They have fused together the bone and there was no sign of infection. But she will be in plaster and then walking with a stick for many months to come. It would have been much better for her prognosis if she'd had treatment within the first few hours of the break."

Dani nodded, knowing there wasn't anything they could have done about that. At least she was alive.

"Will charges be brought against Helen Baxter?" DCS Douglas asked.

Dani shook her head. "We have the sworn testimony of Bernie and Morag that Helen struck Duncan Hart when he was about to bring the axe down on Bernie's neck. Alice Hart may dispute this but the evidence speaks for itself. The axe has Hart's fingerprints all over it. The Fiscal's office are looking at the circumstances, but there's no way they will prosecute Helen."

"We were lucky she was such a brave woman," Douglas added.

"Yes, once the morphine had begun to leave her system, Helen became more wakeful. She could hear there was some kind of altercation going on in the library. Knowing the danger someone could wield with the medicines in the veterinary bag, she felt it was her duty to go and investigate. It took all the energy she had left to lift the poker and drag her wounded leg out into the hallway. From there she saw the terrifying action unfolding."

"Well," Douglas added. "DC Duncan Hart is still in intensive care on a life support system. The doctors have assessed him as essentially brain dead, but his mother is so far refusing to allow the machine to be turned off."

"I suppose it reminds her too much of her husband's fate." James shuddered. "It was an awful thing to have happened back then, not that it excuses the Harts' actions now."

Douglas let out a long breath. "My father told me a policeman had ended up under the wheels of one of the coaches at Ravenscraig, but I hadn't realised he later died from his injuries. It's absolutely tragic."

Dani nodded her agreement. "When Morag understood the full extent of her husband's crimes, she was prepared to tell me everything about what had been going on for the last week."

"It turns out we were all pawns in Bernie's game," James said bitterly.

"Morag knew Bernie had been one of the strikers at Ravenscraig during the strikes of 1984. She was aware of his prison sentence for assault, but he told her the charges were entirely unjustified; the system had conspired against the picketers when all they were doing was defending themselves against police violence."

"It's still what many people believe," Douglas stated. "I'm not denying there was police heavy-handedness, but it went both ways."

"When Bernie received his pardon from the Crown this October, Morag said his reaction was ambivalent. He was pleased to have his named cleared, but it also seemed to reignite his anger against his old foes – the police and the strike-breakers. 'Taff' Shannahan was a man Bernie had kept close over the years, using the information he had over him to get him to skivvy on his building projects. But the fact Taff had been one of the men in those coaches, passing the picket line and in his mind betraying his comrades on the ground, began to build a fresh resentment."

"He had a resentment towards all of us he invited to that house party," James said.

"Oliver told us Bernie had been estranged from his sister for many years and hardly had anything to do with Sasha since she was born. This was because Justine Corder had married another steelworker at Ravenscraig and he had also broken the strike, wanting to have a wage for his new baby daughter. Bernie had never forgiven him, or Justine for standing by him. Cliff had been injured in an accident at the works not long after, but it didn't stop Bernie hating him."

"So he invited Sasha there to punish his sister and brother-in-law in some way?" Sharon was curious. "Did he intend her to be struck by the axe during the target session?"

"Sasha's father is now dead, so it was Justine that Bernie wanted to punish. It was him who sabotaged the target and he made sure Oliver and Sasha were the ones using it, but Morag insists nobody was meant to get hurt. He wanted the axe to miss the target, humiliate and frighten them a bit.

He had no idea it was going to re-bound so far, never mind slash Sasha's forehead."

"She's had her stitches, by the way," James added conversationally. "There's an ointment she can massage into the wound as it heals to minimise the chance of scarring. But she won't know for a while yet if there will be a permanent mark. Oliver and I have been texting."

"She would just have been happy to be reunited with her husband, I expect," Sharon said. "He was lucky to have got out of that house alive. You all were."

"Some of us didn't," Dani added sombrely. "Although that was never Raven's plan. Bernie had lifted a strip of prednisolone pills from Allan's bag when he'd been treating his herd before Christmas. He crushed a few in Jet's food bowl before Oliver and Sasha were due to come down the stairs. Morag says the plan was for Jet's aggression to shake the couple up a bit, give them a fright. The pills were out of his system in a few hours."

"It was like a campaign of terror," Dermot grumbled.

"Tony and Dotty Shannahan had known something was wrong from the beginning. They'd never been invited to join the Ravens for a social gathering before. Tony thought Bernie was going to reveal his secret to his family now living in Ireland, or worse. That's why he took one of the axes when he saw the opportunity. He shoved it in the oversized coat he'd borrowed. When he said he was going to check on his wife when we returned, he hid it under his pillow. It was his insurance policy. It was probably why he didn't bother to lock the door the night he was killed. He was the one with the weapon, after all."

"What did Bernie want with you and James?" Sharon was genuinely puzzled.

Dani glanced at her senior officer before continuing, aware this part of the story was already known to him as they had compared notes as soon as she'd returned from the Highlands. "James had worked for Bernie as a legal consultant on a housing project. He mentioned his partner was called Dani and a senior officer in Police Scotland. It didn't take Bernie and his organisation long to work out it was DCI Danielle Bevan, based at Pitt Street Serious Crime Unit. There aren't many senior female officers in the force."

"I had no idea Bernie would have any interest in you, Dani. I'm so very sorry."

She nodded to acknowledge his words. "Bernie had been keeping tabs on DCS Ronnie Douglas for decades. He'd become obsessed with him. At several points in the last few years Bernie had planned to break into the Douglas's house in Bearsden, perhaps kidnap Mrs Douglas. But their place has security like Fort Knox." Dani smiled wryly, "and the house wasn't designed by Raven Homes."

"But *why*?" Dermot demanded, outraged on behalf of the DCS.

Douglas himself answered this question. "My father was a detective sergeant in 1984. He was one of the officers who were brought in to police the picket line on the 3rd May at Ravenscraig. I knew he'd been caught up in the violent exchanges. But I had no idea that DS Leonard Douglas was the man who arrested Bernard Corder for assault."

Chapter 57

Sharon put a hand up to her mouth. "Your father was the one who put Bernard away for six months in Barlinnie, Sir?"

"Well, he is listed as the arresting officer, obviously the law courts did the rest."

"No wonder Raven had a grudge against you," Dermot commented. "So what was he doing? Trying to even the score sheet with all his old adversaries?"

"Something like that," Dani continued. "When Bernie worked out my next in command was DCS Ronnie Douglas, he looked up some of my cases in the press, he saw us quoted together in several articles and decided we were close colleagues. If he couldn't get to Douglas, he could now get to me."

James's features were drawn with guilt. "He was absolutely insistent I bring Dani for the house party. I should have known something was wrong then."

"How could you have?" Douglas retorted. "We'd no idea who the man was. He'd changed his identity."

"How did he plan to take his revenge?" Sharon asked warily. "Surely he wouldn't have hurt you?"

"I don't think he would have done anything violent with Morag there. She now admits they disconnected the broadband the day we arrived. Like fools we believed they didn't have any. Bernie also left a menacing note under our door on the first night, to get us rattled and paranoid."

"Yes, Jackson picked up on that straightaway. He saw the house had been connected to the highspeed cable last year."

"He's a clever lad. We should have checked that before we even arrived. But it was all so last minute." James ran a hand through his hair.

"With us cut off from the outside world and in the awful weather that the Ravens knew was coming, perhaps they hoped the DCS would come himself to save me. They would have enticed him into their lair."

Dermot furrowed his brow. "I think it was maybe more symbolic than that. Bernie had gathered together representatives from those who he felt had betrayed him; Tony as a strike-breaker, you as a representative of the police who sent him to prison, and Sasha as a symbol of the family who let him down – not just his sister for marrying a *scab*, but his ex-wife and kids too."

Douglas nodded slowly. "I think you may be right Dermot. He'd got you all trapped there on his estate where he could mess with you as he wished. So why were the local vet and his wife invited?"

"According to Morag, Allan Baxter put down Bernie's favourite bull last year. It couldn't be helped, but he'd loathed the man ever since. I also think he wanted to be able to dip into that medicine bag again if possible. Perhaps some cat laxatives in the petit fours." Dani managed a smile.

"So Bernie never set out to kill any of you? Just frighten you a bit and toy with you for his own amusement?" Sharon drained her cup, wondering if she should go out for more and perhaps a box of doughnuts whilst she was there, her stomach was starting to rumble noisily.

"I don't believe Morag would have let him go too far. She knew nothing about the level of Bernie's violence back during the strikes. What she heard on that last night shocked her to the core."

"So Bernie had set out to enjoy a festive week of making us all bloody miserable. But he hadn't counted on Duncan Hart getting wind of his plans," James said.

Dani's expression became deadly serious. "No, he certainly had not."

Chapter 58

The designer holdall, crammed full of clothes they'd bought together in the Boxing Day sales, sat by Jackson's feet.

Sharon scanned the small living room for any items he may have forgotten to pack. "Are you sure you've got your Xbox? Including the controller?"

"Yes," Jackson said with a grin. "I've got all my new toiletries too. I couldn't leave behind my David Beckham deodorant." He shifted awkwardly from one foot to the other. "Thanks for all the stuff you bought, and for having me here, of course."

Sharon had promised herself she wouldn't get emotional, it was the last thing this lad needed. But her throat was tight and tears were threatening to pool in her eyes. "You can thank DCS Douglas's expense account," she joked. "And I've loved having you here. So has DI Muir."

Jackson took a faltering step forward and Sharon grabbed him into an embrace. "Don't be a stranger, eh? I'd like to come and visit from time to time. I haven't taken you to the police museum on Bell Street yet, you'll love it."

The lad gave her a squeeze back. "I promise I will. But it would easier if you got an Xbox account, that's where I do a lot of my socialising."

"Then that's exactly what I will do. I'll go back to the sales on Buchanan Street and shop for an Xbox. Spend my Christmas money."

Jackson laughed. "Cool."

The social worker waiting by the front door tapped her watch. "I need to get him to his mum's new flat by noon," she said gently.

"Yeah, sure," Sharon said, a little too brightly.

Jackson picked up his bag. "We're living in a new place the child protection people found us, but Mum wants us to move far away; just me, her, Emily and Oscar. Maybe somewhere more rural. But I'll let you know, I promise."

Sharon nodded, no longer trusting herself to speak.

He walked towards the door. She turned and gave him a final smile before the social worker led him away. Sharon moved forward and shut the door gently behind them, before sliding to her knees on the carpet and dissolving into wrenching sobs.

Chapter 59

It was New Year's Day and the pub was nearly empty. All the partying had gone on the night before and most of the city's residents were cosy at home, nursing hangovers and watching The Sound of Music on the telly.

Dermot had bought the first round of drinks. He placed a gin and tonic in front of Sharon first. They'd all been tactfully ignoring the puffy redness around her eyes. The cause was no secret. He felt pretty cut up himself. If he was honest, he hadn't been able to face the final goodbye, saying his farewells to the boy at the station, when Jackson had finished the session with the social worker.

Dani and James were both drinking red wine, having refused the offer of a wee drop of single malt to see in the New Year. It was seemingly too much of a reminder of their fateful trip to the Highlands. The DI wondered if they'd ever be comfortable drinking whisky again.

Dani raised her glass. "To teamwork," she declared with a grin.

Dermot sipped his dram. It slipped down very smoothly indeed. "How are you getting on with the evidence gathering?" He asked his boss. "You know, you should really try and take a break, your holiday was hardly a relaxing experience after all."

"No, it certainly wasn't," James added dryly.

"I will. As soon as I'm sure we've got a cast iron case against Bernard Raven and Duncan Hart."

"Hart still hasn't regained consciousness. No sign of brain activity. It may only be Alice who serves any jail time out of those two." James took a gulp of wine.

"How much was Alice Hart involved in the murders?" Sharon asked. "I know she was working there for years as a housekeeper, but wasn't she just gathering information for her son, waiting for the best time for him to strike and wreak his revenge?"

"I've been creating a detailed time-line of events," Dani explained. "When Alice was masquerading as Mrs Noble and we all arrived as guests, like us, she had no way of contacting her son when the broadband had been disconnected. There was the telephone, but if she used that, her conversation could be easily overheard. I think they'd already formulated something of a plan before the guests arrived."

"Strathain House being completely cut off like that in the bad weather gave them one hell of an opportunity to make their move on Bernard," Dermot commented.

"Yes, as housekeeper, she knew most of the plans for Bernie and Morag's little terror campaign against their unsuspecting guests and decided to use it to their advantage. DC Duncan Hart must have been on duty at the police station in Inverlael when I called them about the axe incident. After that, he was biding his time. Then Dr Huntley informed the police that Allan, Sasha and Pete were on their way to seek medical assistance. Hart made sure he was there to greet them all when they arrived at Huntley's surgery, like your local friendly policeman. Alice managed to make a call to his extension and when she knew her son was on his way I think she went out and cut the telephone wire. Morag seemed genuinely shocked when I told her the line was dead."

"Did Hart tell his fellow officers he was planning to go to the house?" Dermot was intrigued.

"Not according to the DI we spoke to. As far as he was concerned, Hart was on leave from the day he met up with the party from the house until the New Year. They'd received a concerned call from DCS Douglas about me being stuck at Strathain, so the Desk Sergeant had requested the utility vehicle from Ullapool to come and help them clear the road. But that didn't arrive until an hour or so after James, Oliver and I got to the station."

"So the local police were never going to get there in time," Dermot said bitterly. "Hart was one step ahead of them."

"Yep, he certainly was. According to Allan Baxter, Hart suggested he accompany Pete Tredegar back to Strathain that afternoon. The irony is that he and Sasha were relieved, they were pleased another police officer would be there to look after their other halves."

"Bastard," James muttered into his glass. "Poor Pete never made it back."

"Tredegar had no idea Hart was a danger to him. Why would he? About halfway along the route back to the house from Inverlael, the DC must have taken him completely by surprise. He must have asked to borrow the pick-axe, under the pretence of breaking the ice under his feet, and when Pete was walking ahead, he sunk the axe head into his back, through the shoulder blades, then dragged his body up the hill and left it in the snow, knowing nobody would be along that path for days."

"Why did the groundsman have to die? He was completely innocent in all this, wasn't he?" Sharon asked, her gin and tonic drained down to the slice of lemon.

"Yes, he was innocent. Bernie had genuinely employed him to help set up the estate for wealthy visitors to 'hunt, shoot and fish'. Hart killed him purely because he was a strong, healthy man with survival skills who would probably want to protect his employer. He needed to be got out of the way."

"Pete also had a backpack full of distress flares, which Hart had plans for," James's expression was solemn.

"I believe that when Hart reached the house, after killing Pete, he went straight to the kitchen door. He waited until his mother was alone and knocked on the glass. He told her of his plan. He would set a flare off in the woods which she would make sure she saw and could tell the rest of us about. Some of our group would be bound to go and investigate. This would give the housekeeper an opportunity to take the key to the medical bag from Helen and hide the bag itself in her room. I expect Hart's mother couldn't believe her luck when Helen came into the kitchen to get a glass of water on her own. She followed her upstairs and when Helen came back out of the bedroom and stood at the top step, Alice gave her a good shove."

"You think it was Alice Hart who pushed Helen Baxter and took the key?" Dermot was intrigued.

"Oh I'm certain, but without a confession from either of them, I can't prove it, beyond the medical bag being found in her room."

James shook his head in frustration. "DC Hart was the one who went upstairs to try and find the medical bag, telling us it wasn't there. In fact, it was in his mother's bedroom all the time. He probably even pocketed the barbiturates and syringe whilst he was up there. We were fools to believe him."

"He was a real policeman," Dani added gravely. "We are conditioned to do as they say. It's a terrible breach of trust when someone uses that authority to commit murder. He will need to be seen to be punished for his crimes and his record as a policeman investigated."

"If he never regains consciousness, will there ever be a trial?" Sharon enquired, not knowing the legal position on this.

"Alice Hart will be put on trial, probably for GBH, attempted murder and conspiracy to murder. In the process, the other details should come out."

James finished his wine. "I wonder why Hart brought down the medicines for Helen? Wasn't he planning to kill us all later anyway?"

Dani sighed. "Having the idea to send us all back to our rooms so the attacker could return the medicines needed to keep Helen alive was Hart's opportunity to sneak into Tony's room and poison him. Helen was out for the count in the drawing room so he could come and go as he pleased during the night. Dotty slept through it all, but I'm sure if she'd woken, he'd have killed her too. But I think they didn't want too much collateral damage. Helen was only injured to get the key, the Harts had no grudge against her. I suspect he left the medicines on the hall table out of a genuine desire to help her."

"Then it was his undoing, because it was Helen who put a stop to him in the end." James put down his glass. "Anyone for another?"

They all nodded.

"I'll go," Sharon declared, pushing back her chair. "Dermot can help me carry them back. Same again?"

When the pair were at the bar, James slipped his hand into Dani's. "Would Hart and his mother really have given Morag that lethal injection and then killed both Dotty and Helen as witnesses? If we'd still been in the house, would he have killed us too?"

Dani shrugged. "Getting Bernie to confess and killing him was their main aim. I think the fact Tony was also there, a man who had been in the coach that crushed Duncan's father, who in his weakness had served Bernie for decades afterwards, was too tempting to resist. I expect Hart enjoyed murdering him. But they never killed Morag when they had the chance, did they? I think they would have left Helen and Dotty alone too, if they'd butchered Bernie with the axe. As far as they were concerned, neither were witnesses to the event."

"They weren't really master criminals, just opportunists," James theorised. "How far would they have got in the snow if they did kill Bernie? They probably never really expected to get away. They knew they'd die in prison."

"Well, their lives had been ended when Duncan's father and Alice's husband died thirty seven years ago. For them, time had stood still. The intervening years had simply been about finding ways to exact their revenge."

James squeezed her hand tighter. They sat in silence waiting for their drinks to arrive.

*

Sharon asked the barman for a tray, placing the four brimming glasses on its polished surface.

"See, you didn't really need me at all," Dermot said with a wink.

"Oh yes I did. You're carrying the snacks."

Dermot laughed, he should have known. He ordered a few packets of nuts and turned to his colleague with a more serious expression. "How are you doing, really?"

She shrugged. "We only knew him less than a week. I'll get over it."

"Sometimes that's all it takes."

Sharon smiled, surprised to feel a rush of heat give her cheeks a pink glow. "How are things with Serena? Did she give you a hard time for the trip to Tenerife?"

"She's not talking to me right now," Dermot muttered. "I'm being ghosted for my sins."

Sharon pulled a face. "What? No phone messages, or anything?"

He shook his head solemnly.

"Oh dear, well, let's hope you're not in the dog house for too long," she said this without much conviction.

Dermot followed Sharon back to the table. He was secretly thinking quite the opposite. Not being bombarded by passive aggressive messages and voicemails from his fiancé had actually been the best start to the New Year he could have wished for.

The End

© Katherine Pathak, The Garansay Press 2021

If you enjoyed this novel, please take a few moments to write a brief review. Reviews really help to introduce new readers to my books and this allows me to keep on writing.
Many thanks,

Katherine.

If you would like to find out more about my books and read my reviews and articles then please visit my blog, TheRetroReview at:

www.KatherinePathak.wordpress.com

To find out about new releases and special offers follow me on Twitter:

@KatherinePathak

Most of all, thanks for reading!

If you enjoyed this book, have you read the others in the DCI Dani Bevan series?

Against A Dark Sky

Book 1 in the DCI Dani Bevan series

They died thirty years ago, but the case is not closed…

Five walkers set out to climb Ben Lomond on a fine October day. Within hours, the weather has taken a turn for the worst. The group find themselves lost on the mountain. Two of the climbers manage to make it back down and call for help.
The following day a body is found. One of the female climbers has been strangled and another man is missing without trace.
DCI Dani Bevan is called to the Loch Lomond town of Ardyle to lead the case. It quickly becomes clear that Bevan must dig into the events of a similar tragedy which occurred on the hills thirty years earlier in order to find the killer.
This investigation requires the DCI to face up to the ghosts of her own tragic past, and to endeavour to put them behind her, once and for all.

On A Dark Sea

Book 2 in the DCI Dani Bevan series

A missing girl.

A broken marriage.

Who can you trust?

When fourteen year old Maisie Riddell goes missing from a Glasgow High School, DCI Dani Bevan knows she needs to act fast, particularly as the Headmistress is the wife of her DS, Phil Boag. But as the inquiry into the girl's disappearance deepens, Bevan finds herself caught in the fall-out from a broken marriage, unsure of whose word she can really trust. The DCI is required to take her search to Norway, in order to discover the truth about Maisie's secret life.

Meanwhile, Bill Hutchison's unauthorised investigation into a brutal murder in Stonehaven places him in terrible danger. With Dani wrapped up in the Riddell case, who is there left to help him...?

A Dark Shadow Falls

Book 3 in the DCI Dani Bevan series

Never invite evil into your home...

DCI Dani Bevan finds herself dragged into the disturbing case of Eric Fisher, a man accused of slaughtering his own family in a case of domestic homicide. But when a spate of violent burglaries breaks out in the area, whilst Fisher is on remand, Dani wonders if the man's claims of innocence are as crazy as they first thought.
The DCI quickly becomes caught up in a race against time to stop a terrifying serial killer, who appears to be one step ahead of Dani's every move.

A Dark Shadow Falls is perhaps the darkest of all the DCI Bevan investigations. It is a police procedural which uncovers dark secrets and a deadly obsession with the bloodiest episodes in Scottish history.

There are 13 books in the series so far, all available from Amazon!

Printed in Great Britain
by Amazon